# Stick and Bones

## by

## Phil Geusz

Published by
Melange Books, LLC
White Bear Lake, MN 55110
**www.melange-books.com**

# Stick and Bones
# By Phil Geusz

Can a slave be freed entirely by the efforts of others? Or must he free himself, lest the chains remain locked around his heart?

Simeon Bolivar carries the taint of slavery in every cell of his body—he's been genetically engineered to serve as unpaid labor and hope for nothing more. He's also the teen-aged son of two of the leaders of the Uprising that in theory set him free. But his parents were murdered on the brink of true victory and his people continue to live half-free in a broken society plagued by slums, drugs and murderous gangs. Does Simeon have what it takes to finish his parent's work and bring about true freedom? Or will his people fester in their hell-hole forevermore?

\* \* \* \*

Author Website
www.resistingarrest.net
\* \* \* \*

**Also at www.melange-books.com by Phil Geusz**

No Glory Sought, Book 1: "No Oath Sworn"
No Glory Sought, Book 2: "No Battle Fought"
No Glory Sought, Book 3: "No Victory Won"

**Stories in Anthologies**

Hearts of Tomorrow: "December Moth"
Paranormal Dreams: "Hell's Angel"

# Chapter One

In some things, the secret to success is pure timing.

I didn't have much use for chink-shops. Still, they could be fun sometimes. I was just shooting up a bunch of T-Men as Pretty Boy Floyd when Peckerhead came and knocked on my cell door. "It's time, Gade."

"Sheee-it," I murmured, killing the holo-sim. I was about to waste Melvin Purvis and win it all; wasn't that a helluva time to have to go to work? But schedules were schedules, and I was the one who was always bitching about how things needed to happen as planned. American Crimelord was a great chinkgame, but not worth screwing up a real job over.

Peckerhead smiled knowingly as I emerged from the holocell, his expression fading when he saw the ice in my eyes. He and I might be cool when it came time to sit around and talk shit, but right now business was calling. He knew by now that I didn't take any crap from anyone when it came time for business. Not even him. "Weiner's already inside," he explained as he fell in alongside me. "And Romeo's found us a ride."

As we left the chinkshop and swung out onto Ninth Street, I kept my eyes open. Not for cars, but to make sure the Ninth Street Avengers were still hanging tight with me. It was habit, was all; Sammy cut them in on everything he did, and I was sort of counting on their help later in the day. But one could never be too sure about these things. I scanned the street twice for their watchman before picking out Doolie's tall, thin greyhound-morph form leaning so close up against an old telephone pole he blended into it. He was a good watchman; honest and true both to his masters and to everyone else he dealt with. It was a dog thing, I supposed. Dogs never had trouble finding work. I nodded slightly as our eyes met, and he even smiled a little. I was glad that I was cool with the Avengers; if Doolie ever decided he didn't like me, I wouldn't last long. So long as you were all right with the Avengers, you didn't have shit else to worry about so long as you were in their territory. No one dared fuck with you or yours; anyone who even thought about doing that kind of shit without the Avengers' blessing would likely as not end up frozen to the sidewalk some cold morning with their balls stuffed down their throat. The Avengers' territory was rich; there were two little stores in it that sold food and shit, plus the chinkshop, a little nightclub, and even (of all things!) an actual doctor's office. There wasn't another gang half so well off anywhere I knew of. That was why Sammy stayed cool with them, where he could've paid anyone. He only dealt with quality. Romeo was just around the corner on Pine Street, leaning up against a lamppost and trying to look as lean and hard as Doolie. He wasn't very good at it; like all of us rabbits he was short and tubby and not very big in the arms and shoulders. Dogs had been gengineered to fight; we rabbits were designed to shut up and perform stoop-labor without making any trouble about it. I smirked at the thought; the whole fuckin' world knew how that one had come out! "Gade," Romeo greeted me, nodding slightly. He was shivering a bit, like he always did when the shit was about to hit the fan. My friend thrived on action.

"You got something for me?" I asked, smiling. I liked Romeo, even though he was a hopeless pincushion and wasted his entire take buying more shit. So long as he wasn't stuck too badly, however, you could count on him all the way to the fucking hilt.

He nodded. "I do. It's an old four- door beater, but the motor's good enough. It's parked just outside the grocery store, where you wanted it to be." He smiled again. "The owner's a fat norm pawnbroker."

My eyes lit up. I'd do what I had to do regardless, but a fat norm pawnbroker was about as good as it got. He stole from us furs every fucking day of the week; why shouldn't we take him for a little ride in return? "Way cool!" I answered. "You got your jack?"

He smiled and pulled a little black box about halfway out of his pants pockets. "Always."

"Outstanding," I answered. I'd been a little worried; Romeo never settled on which car to steal until the very last minute. It would've been annoying, except that he always had about a million good reasons for being so picky. Then I turned to Peckerhead. "And you say Weiner's

6

already inside? That's for sure?"

"Oh, yeah!" my number-two man agreed, nodding hard.

I nodded back. Peckerhead was valuable for many reasons, but the most important was that he had a legitimate job Outside as a parking lot attendant. It was all just bullshit, really; he didn't make hardly anything at all. But bullshit or no, it gave him plenty of time to just sit and look around and pay attention to shit without anyone seeing anything strange about it.

Leaving the Zone was a snap; Sammy made up fake work-passes for us whenever we needed them, no questions asked. So long as we wore cheapshit work clothes and kept our eyes low and subservient, no one ever gave us any crap. We hit the gates right at shift-change time, merging in with the other furs headed out to work legitimate gigs as maids, gardeners, factory-slaves, and all the other low-class jobs the norms were too fucking good to do for themselves. They'd tried to make us work for free, once upon a time—fucking *owned* us! But then we went apeshit on them one fine June morning, and they learned that they didn't own quite as much of us as they thought. My mother and father had been among the leaders, in charge of our whole city. Like most of their peers, they didn't survive the experience. I couldn't even remember them, I'd been so little. Because of what they'd done, though, the furs always gave me a little extra respect. Which was plenty cool by me.

"Down that way, Gade," Romeo whispered in my ear. "The blue one."

"Right," I agreed. A big police-snake was wrapped around the traffic signal at the corner, its ugly four-camera head taking in everything around it. The fuckers carried microphones too, and Sammy had warned me since I was little that they could hear a gnat fart. Police-snakes were harder than shit to fox, which left only one viable alternative. I felt inside my jacket; the packets were still there, all right. I'd only checked about a million times. Then I looked at my watch; everything was still cool. "We're on," I confirmed.

I didn't know who or what monitored the police snakes; it wasn't important, so I'd never bothered to find out. What I did know was that the things defended themselves with tasers. These wouldn't be a problem. Keeping our eyes low and servile, Peckerhead and I let Romeo fall back a little ways, so he'd be right alongside his targeted car when we put in the fix.

"Move!" I ordered, my voice clear and calm like it always was at moments like these. With a single fluid motion, we pulled out our cable-guns...

...and instantly the snake came to life. "Freeze!" it ordered, the blue lights mounted on its head suddenly flashing. "You are—"

But it never finished. As one, we fired at the sewer lid almost under our feet. By the time the snake's taser-darts struck us, the superconductors in our ordinary-looking clothing were so firmly grounded that all the electricity in the North American power grid couldn't touch us. Sure, the darts stung. But who gave a shit, so long as we were still up and moving?

"You are—" the snake repeated. But I wasn't having any of it. I fired my cable-gun again, this time grounding the body of the snake itself so it couldn't shock me directly. Then I pulled out three stickybags full of Sammy's best home-made thermite and slapped them onto the snake's body. The last one I flung up as high as I could; it stuck just below the head.

"We're in!" Romeo cried out just as I punched my detonator-remote. Sammy mixed his explosives in several different ways; this batch was intended to ignite rather than blow up. Still, the shit burned damn fast and the snake was deader than fuck before Peckerhead and I had dashed the few steps back to our stolen ride.

"Those snakes cost, like, a bazillion dollars," Romeo observed as he plugged his 'jack into the car's diagnostic socket. Multicolored lights flashed on the dashboard as the onboard computer fought and lost its last battle, then everything went green and Romeo was in charge. He powered us up and then eased us into the traffic lane and around the remains of the police snake, which was now little more than a pile of molten metal oozing its way deep into the asphalt. "You'd think it'd be cheaper if they just let us *have* the fuckin' car!"

"Heh!" Peckerhead agreed. Then he pulled out a stick and injected himself. "That's for the shakes, Gade," he explained before I could object. "I'm hurtin', man!"

I frowned, but said nothing. Pecker and Romeo were both pincushions, and that was that. They'd be hooked until the shit eventually killed them. Which was just as well, I supposed. If they hadn't needed the money for drugs, they probably wouldn't be desperate enough to help me pull off these crazy jobs. Besides, what the fuck else was there in this messed-up world for furs like them? I'd have been a pincushion myself if Sammy hadn't been shooting me up with counters every week since I was almost a baby. Counters were nasty; if someone taking them tried to shoot up with stick, he got sicker than hell. Not that I ever found out for myself. Sammy pulled samples too, and told me the first time I came up dirty he'd put me out in the cold. That was too terrible to even think about. And besides, stick didn't look so cool anymore. I was beginning to think you had to be a hugely stupid motherfucker to even try the shit.

All three of us kept a close lookout as we cruised through NormTown, though we didn't see a thing. A police-beetle screamed towards the grave of its brother-in-arms, but it didn't even glance at us. Taking down a beetle was a lot harder than burning a snake; it took either serious firepower or a lot of preplanning. By five-thirty we were sitting two blocks away from Universal Check-Cashing, an outfit I'd been casing for weeks. It was Friday, and the place was swamped with just-paid furs and even a few norms either so fucking broke, desperate or stupid they'd willingly give up ten percent for cash now, where any sane person would open up a bank account and then get to keep it all when the check cleared on Wednesday. I felt a little sorry for them anyway, even though I knew most of them were hurting because of stick or liquor or gambling or too much time in the chinkshop. They were victims, in the greater scheme of things.

But the owner of the check-cashing place... Who felt sorry for *him*? Certainly not me.

"Weiner's inside for sure," Peckerhead offered, even though I hadn't asked. "I watched our friend carry the bag in."

I nodded; Weiner was a tiny fuck, one the smallest bunnies I'd ever known. He stood only about two feet high and his back was hunched over so much that he had to get around on all fours. Sammy told me once that he was a throwback, a partial reversion to the original rabbit-form, and he'd made me read a big, thick book on gengineering. But unlike most throwbacks, Weiner's mind was fine. Or at least his mind was fine when it wasn't all whacked out. He used way too damn much stick. I'd had to put an entire unused syringe in the suitcase with him to make sure he wouldn't go into withdrawal before the time was right. Weiner was the weakest spot in the whole plan, but what could I do? Where else was I gonna find a two-foot-tall quadrupedal bunny willing to sit in a rented locker all day and wait? Especially one who was also the slickest, fastest escape-artist I'd ever seen?

Suddenly an alarm bell rang. "This is it!" I said, even though I didn't need to. It was as if a switch had been flipped in the stolen car; suddenly we were all business.

"Yeah," Romeo agreed, his ears rising in interest despite himself. Normally Romeo was a honey-brown color, but he'd dyed himself black for this job. Me and Peckerhead had too, though I rather hoped we hadn't missed as many spots on the backs of our ears as he had. The bell rang and rang, and gradually the dull-witted check-cashers began to grasp that something was wrong. Their heads swung about uneasily and those equipped with mobile ears raised them. Suddenly, a swirl erupted in the crowd. I knew it was Weiner, down on all fours and carrying a moneybag of some kind or another in his mouth. Sure enough, an instant after the swirl passed through a bunch of guard-dogs appeared, brandishing blast-rifles and looking pissed. I smiled to myself. As small and low and chase-smart as he was, Weiner would never offer a rifleman a clear line of fire. Whoever set up Universal's security hadn't considered the possibility of an inside job by a tiny, fast-moving quadruped, and who could blame them?

Then things started to go wrong. Another uniformed guard-dog emerged, this one a greyhound like Doolie back with the Avengers. Greyhound-morphs had been cooked up specifically to hunt down us rabbits; this was bad news indeed. "Shit!" Romeo observed.

I frowned, too. We hadn't known Universal had a greyhound on staff; it'd be just our fucking luck if this was his first day. Still, I'd considered the possibility. "Weiner's goddamn fast," I pointed out. "He'll make it this far."

"Maybe," Peckerhead replied. He leaned forward a little. "Be a helluva show if he gets caught."

I curled my lips in disgust; Peckerhead enjoyed blood vids and was a big fangfight fan. It was unusual for a rabbit to develop a carnivore's taste for gore, but somehow he'd managed.

"There!" Romeo observed as Weiner leapt extra-high over a car, eyes wide in terror and green cash-bag clamped tightly in his teeth. He couldn't have any idea how much money he'd stolen; the bag might contain twenties or fifties or even just blank accounting-slips meant for the bookies that always could be found at check-cashing places. His part of the operation was simply to break out of his locker and grab whatever he thought he could get away with. Though the more he stole, the more he'd be allowed to keep.

"And there!" Peckerhead added, pointing at the big greyhound as it vaulted over the same car, perhaps a second behind our friend.

"He'll make it," I declared, a bit more confidently than I felt. I rolled down the car's window and hung my head out. I'd have exactly one, and only one, chance to pull this off.

Sure enough, here came Weiner exactly according to plan and schedule, barreling down the narrow sidewalk for all he was worth. Obediently he dropped his bag on the sidewalk—

—and instantly I threw the door wide-open directly into the path of the oncoming greyhound.

*WHAM!* The dog slammed into the door like the end of the world, full-bore and headfirst, then dropped to the concrete without so much as a whimper. The impact slammed the door shut again, hard. So I re-opened it and scooped up the loot as Weiner, blown and exhausted, doubled back and hopped in alongside me.

"All right!" Peckerhead exulted as he slapped his wheezing friend on the back. "All *right!*"

Romeo was smiling too as he powered up the car and got ready to pull out into traffic. But he didn't move us an inch. For the real game was only just beginning. It'd taken me weeks to plan this job, and Sammy'd sunk a lot of resources into it as well. My cohorts might be perfectly happy with a quarter-share of a bag that might or might not be filled with cash in return for so much risk and toil, but I certainly wasn't.

Not when there were far more valuable items at hand for the taking.

I'd chosen our waiting-spot very carefully indeed; while the check-cashing guards might guess that a getaway car was involved, we were far enough away that they could only guess which one of dozens we might be waiting in. Plus, their building was brightly-lit while we were lurking in the shadows. On top of that, the theft had been a small one, relatively speaking. It wouldn't make sense to denude the main treasure of most of its guards in order to chase a single cash-bag. So as anticipated no one else followed to support the greyhound, who now lay unconscious amid his widely-scattered teeth. Instead, like anyone else would do, they waited for the police-snake at the intersection to come to life and call for backup. Its blue lights had long-since turned themselves on, and the beast was even now tracking bunny-spoor down the sidewalk.

"Come on..." I whispered under my breath. It was very hard indeed to just sit and wait at the scene of a crime instead of instantly fleeing as my lapine ancestors had for so many thousands of generations before me. "Come on..."

Then it happened. The same police-beetle that'd investigated the death of the snake we'd killed earlier came roaring up. Because we'd left it only a few blocks away it was the first responder, and even more importantly it was travelling all by itself, along a predictable route. Romeo might've been a pincushion, but he could drive like a motherfucker. The car had been waiting in reverse-gear for over a minute; now he goosed the throttle and rammed us ass-backwards into the speeding beetle. *WHAM!* The impact was a lot worse than when the dog hit the door; I'd been worried we'd be knocked silly. But Sammy had predicted there'd be no problem and as always he was right. Little Weiner was thrown pretty hard, but didn't give a shit. All he cared about was the fresh stick waiting for him in the floorboards.

Instead of stopping after hitting the beetle, Romeo kept his foot mashed flat to the floor so that, skidding and protesting all the way, the beetle was forced out of the street and down the alley across the way. The car steered funny with the beetle locked to its bumper but somehow Romeo managed, only striking the wall a couple of glancing blows along the way. The alley was a dead-end, and as instructed my driver rammed the beetle into the wall hard at the end, kicking up a shower of sparks I hoped was the nasty thing's primary batteries shorting out.

"All right!" I declared, hopping out and lighting my minitorch. Now was my time. The turret was trying to deploy itself, though the mechanism was too fucked up from the collision for it to operate, again just as planned. Beetles weren't armored, though I hadn't a clue as to why not; if I'd designed the fuckers they sure as hell would've been. So it took only a few seconds to slice open the sheet metal and access the innards of the beast. There were five black boxes, just as Sammy had told me there'd be. With a quick snip-snip, they became mine. Then I slashed through the gun-mount, tipped the whole thing over on top of the stolen car's ruined trunk and finally tack-welded it into place. People would notice, yes. But we had less than a mile to go before we hit the river, and with any luck even the police-snakes wouldn't be able to do anything more than watch us race by and ram through the barbed-wire. Once we got there the Ninth Street Avengers would be waiting for us with open arms. Sammy could make cheap-shit stenguns all day long, sure enough. But a police -issue machine-cannon was another story entirely. This was worth all the time, risk, and effort we'd poured into the operation, and more. Not a tiny bag of maybe-cash.

"All right!" I declared one last time as I hopped back into the half-ruined getaway car and slapped the dashboard. "If this piece of shit'll just get us back to the Zone, you guys can party all fucking week long, my treat."

# Chapter Two

If I'd been stupid the way most criminals are, I wouldn't have gone home and cleaned the black dye out of my fur before going out to party. Peckerhead, Weiner and Romeo might or might not have figured out to wash up on their own, they being a notch or two above average despite the stick-thing, but I made damn sure they knew what to do, regardless.

The Zone was too dangerous and expensive to be worth policing as a general rule, but that didn't mean there wouldn't be any heat or snitches at all. The cops tended to sit up and take notice when machine-cannons went missing, especially when it was the law enforcement community you lifted them from in the first place. The government wasn't barred from policing a Zone, Sammy had explained to me more than once. They merely weren't obliged to. Auto-cannon theft was precisely the kind of thing that might make the fat cats reconsider their cost-benefit ratios.

So, instead of going straight out onto the dance floor when I passed through the front door of The Warrens, I turned right, smiled up at the armed feline guard that stood on watch twenty-four-seven, and went all the way down to the very end of the long corridor, past the little private rooms the nightclub often rented out to those blessed with heavy wallets. The hallway made a sharp left turn, and a red line was painted on the floor. A little sign posted there promised mayhem and worse to anyone who passed that spot; it emphasized the point with a little skull-and-crossbones. Sammy had an autosecurity system set up there salvaged and modified from an obsolete-model police snake. It was programmed to let me pass, and in truth I didn't even think about the setup much anymore except when I had to step over a body to get where I was going. Sammy was a stand-up guy, for the most part. But he didn't fuck around regarding security, and who could blame him? He owned the biggest gold mine in the Zone. Or maybe he was the biggest gold mine; I never could quite decide.

The hallway soon became a flight of downward-leading stairs. I stopped on the seventh one and bounced up and down twice in place to activate the hidden switch. I had to be careful since one bounce would set off every alarm and booby-trap in the universe, while three times was the signal that I'd led someone home under duress. A loud click snapped and then the stair-tread behind me rose, revealing Sammy's carefully-camouflaged lair.

"Simeon!" he greeted me, looking up from his workbench. The Ninth Street Avengers had delivered his new toy and, predictably, it was already half-disassembled. "I'm so glad you're home." His smile widened. "Excellent work, son. Magnificent, even! I'm so proud!"

I shouldn't have felt the way I did about Sammy. He wasn't my real dad, after all. And he made me do all kinds of embarrassing shit like go to school, read books and exercise. He was even a fucking norm, one of the handful still living in the Zone. I had every reason to resent the shit out of him. But somehow, what Sammy thought mattered a lot deep-down inside me. I felt my ear-linings darken in the lapine equivalent of a blush. "I planned it, like, forever. It was *supposed* to go well."

"Ha!" Sammy answered, lowering his head to peer at me over the top of his granny-glasses. He wasn't just a Norm but an old fart to boot. He wore his mostly-gray hair long, in a ponytail, and sported a big bushy beard besides. "It was a fine, successful operation, Simeon." He patted his new cannon lovingly. "I've wanted one of these for years."

I sighed and shook my head as I walked across Sammy's work area and back to the little room I called my own. Not that it was much of a room; our hidey-hole had once been a public fallout shelter and whoever designed it hadn't been much for interior walls. I'd made myself an enclosure out of empty crates and then hung a curtain across the entrance for privacy. The stacks didn't reach all the way to the ceiling, so every time Sammy used a power-tool the racket was enough to wake the dead. It was still better than his little bunk-area, however, and he never complained even though we were perpetually short on floor space.

Our lair was close enough to the edge of the Zone to have running water; Sammy'd tapped a water main years ago for both us and the nightclub, and the resulting flow helped pay our rent. So I was able to take my time in the shower getting the black dye out of my fur. It was pretty nasty shit. Sammy made it from a recipe in one of his books. But it would wash out if encouraged enough. At least I had plenty of soap to help me; my friends probably didn't, and I couldn't imagine what they must be going through. Plus I even had a working blow-dryer. I was King Shit by Zone standards, I supposed. That made me just about the biggest loser in the universe, compared to most norms Outside. They all had yachts, I mused as I ran the hot air back and forth over myself. The dryer always made me sleepy and thoughtful. Yachts that floated back and forth over pretty blue lakes. They were ringed with big green trees and birds that sang real honest-to-god songs instead of just shitting all over the—

"...done yet, Simeon?" Sammy was asking from the other side of my curtain, I suddenly realized. "We need to talk some more."

I sighed and turned off the dryer. Try though I might, I'd never been able to get Sammy to call me "Gade". He didn't seem to like my nickname. When my friends used it in front of him, sometimes his face even screwed up a little. "Sure. What about?"

"This," he answered, pulling aside my curtain and laying my essay on the desk he'd scrounged for me so long ago that I could hardly remember. He frowned, and fingered the numerous red ink marks on the cover page. "Son, I know you've been busy on the job..."

"Jesus!" I complained, looking up towards heaven. "What the fuck do you *want* out of me, Sammy? I'm the best jobber you've got, and we both damn well know it. Plus, I ain't so bad with the shop equipment either. Even you say so! I'm pulling my weight. When are you gonna stop treating me like a baby?"

"*Not* so bad with the shop equipment," Sammy corrected me, and I rolled my eyes in pain. "*Not* so bad." He scowled. "Look. I know you've got to learn to survive on the street. You *have* to, being who and what you are. So you can't help but pick up the mindset. But I keep telling you... There's so much *more* out there!"

I looked down at my much marked-up essay—about the cultural impact of the Industrial Revolution on western civilization. "There ain't another bunny in the Zone gotta do this shit." I protested.

"There ain't another bunny in the Zone could've planned and pulled off that job today, either. Don't you think that just maybe the one might have something to do with the other?" Sammy suddenly frowned. "Isn't another bunny, rather. Now you've got me doing it."

I smiled despite myself, then Sammy did too. He shook his head. "Look, Simeon. Maybe I am asking too much. But..." He met my eyes. "Tell me you didn't enjoy doing the research for this paper."

I looked away. "That part," I admitted, "was fun."

Sammy smiled. "Yep, I thought so. And despite all the crappy grammar you didn't do a bad job. I especially liked how you compared the Uprising to the general European social upheaval of 1848." He tilted his head to one side. "That was *good*, Simeon."

I felt my ears blush again. "They both had lotsa causes," I explained. "Too many to really understand. And both of them pretty much went nowhere, in the greater scheme of things."

"Maybe nowhere, maybe not," Sammy answered, not specifying which revolution he was referring to. Then he shrugged. "Anyway... If you'd use proper grammar you'd really be somewhere. Well ahead of most kids your age. Far ahead, even."

I looked away. "Why should I talk shit, just 'cause all you Norms do?"

Sammy sighed and looked away. "There is that, I suppose. From your point of view." Then he picked up the report and tossed it into my lap. "You get an 'A' for content, an 'A' for reasoning skills, and a 'D' for grammar. Try not to use the word 'fuck' anymore in formal writing. All right, Simeon? Can you at least give me *that* much?"

I rolled my eyes. It was all quite deliberate. Including the mangled sentences, as Sammy knew perfectly well. It'd seemed cool at the time. But now... "Yes sir."

Then my guardian smiled and everything seemed all better, just like it always had since I was little. He reached out and tousled my ears, something I'd pull a shiv over if anyone else tried it. "I'm glad to hear it, son. The world's done nothing but piss on you from before the day you were born, so it stands to reason that there's going to be a few rough spots in your character. Still... Your parents were something special, Simeon. Every day you remind me more and more of them." He turned to leave. "They'd be proud, son. Of both the report, and the job, so well done. Why don't you take the weekend off? All work and no play makes Simeon a dull bunny, after all."

# Chapter Three

A whole weekend off! I'd intended to take a break anyway, but this was even better than I'd expected. Planning a job was hard work, and the essay hadn't been any cakewalk either. None of my friends ever worked so hard at anything. In fact, most of them thought I was out of my fuckin' mind not to party more, as rich as I was compared to them. Life's short, they kept telling me, and it wasn't gonna stop raining shit anytime soon in the Zone. So why shouldn't I spend more time being happy and living large?

Even just a year or two ago, that line had sounded pretty convincing. All the really cool people went for it, to one degree or another, and bought the stick that I now understood was what was really being sold. And sure enough, one by one they turned thin and sickly and brittle-furred. They even quit growing, which was all the more tragic for us rabbits since we were so undersized to start with. The users might live large, but they wouldn't live long. Sammy claimed the stick dealers were even bigger Enemies of the People than the Imperialist norms outside the Zone, but he didn't dare lift a finger against them. They were entrenched too deeply into the Zone's power-structure and economy. Even the Ninth Street Avengers, if forced to choose between Sammy and stick, would choose the needle every time. Sammy paid well, but they *needed* drugs.

Since I didn't do the pincushion thing, there was exactly one way left for me to have a good time. It was almost nine before I made my way up the stairs and back into The Warrens, which meant things were only just getting started. Our neighborhood, like all Zone neighborhoods, was made up mostly of rabbit-folk. So the band played heavy-beat Hop music of the kind we lapines mostly liked. The Rope was working guard duty;

he took a moment to smile at me as I eased past him and out onto the dance floor, white fangs flashing in his dark face. I kinda liked The Rope, even though he wasn't half as smart as he thought he was. The big feline read a few books now and then, and therefore knew a little bit about a few things. We'd talk, and I'd begin to believe that I might've finally found someone besides Sammy who'd heard of, say, the Revolutions of 1848. But then he'd say something incredifuckingly stupid and make himself look like a total idiot. Tonight was to be no exception. "Adolph Hitler did too kill George Washington!" he declared in-between wanding guests and collecting cover charges. He had to raise his voice to do it; the music was loud, loud, loud, just the way I liked it.

"You're full of shit, Gade! I read about it when I was little, in a picture book!"

Probably a picture book starring Superman, I decided for about the thousandth time as I smiled back and shook my head in a friendly way. The Rope meant well, I knew. And by Zone standards he was a friggin' genius just by being literate. But in his mental universe the pyramids were built by the UFO-men and the Declaration of Independence was being signed at about the same time the Jews were dying in Dachau. And what the fuck could you do with someone like that? Give him a brainless job wanding down drug dealers and their wannabees, I supposed, at shit wages in a crappy Zone-club with no future and no hope of things ever getting any better, while all the time he insisted he was the only one who knew the true way of things. The real heartbreaker was that his mind was among the best the Zone had to offer!

"Hey! It's the Gade!" a new voice interrupted. Without my even noticing him, Spunk, whose birth-name was George, had eased up on my right. He was a sneaky one, Spunk was; most of the time my survival instincts would've warned me before he was within striking range. Not that I was afraid of little Spunk shanking me or anything; far from it. We'd played together when we were little. Besides, he didn't have a tenth the balls it'd take. Sammy wouldn't be happy if anything bad happened to me. Not happy at all.

"Georgie," I replied, smiling and slapping my long-ago friend on the back. It was cool to call someone by their real name sometimes if you'd known them when they were little. "How're they hangin', rabbit-brother mine?"

"I'm keepin' on keepin' on," he replied easily from behind his thick, dark glasses. He wore them indoors, I knew, because eventually stick made a user's eyes overly sensitive to light. In the latter stages of the addiction, that was. When death wasn't just a distant theoretical possibility anymore. His smile intensified. "I hear the Renegade scored big today!"

I pressed my lips together and looked away. On the one hand, Spunk might simply be taking a normal interest in the exploits of an old friend. But on the other, he had to pay for his stick somehow. Information was always good currency. Would a hurting doper sell out an old friend for his next fix? *Fuck*, yes! Coldly and without hesitation. Stick was nasty shit! "Maybe," I answered, shrugging and turning towards the dance floor.

"Aw, come on!" Spunk replied. "I hear you scored heavy, man! Biggest fucking haul in years, direct from the pigs to Sammy's garage."

I kept walking, but Spunk didn't get the hint. "Was it an autocannon?" he demanded. Then his eyes narrowed and he asked the important question, the one that told me for sure he wasn't my friend anymore. "Who's Sammy gonna sell it to? The Avengers?"

That was quite enough. I stopped cold, then reached into my pocket and pulled out a five-credit coin. "Here," I declared, throwing it down on the floor. It rolled, and behind the dark glasses I watched Spunk's eyes follow it greedily. "Go buy your fix and get the fuck out of my life." He went scampering after the coin as intently as a hungry puppy pursues his dam, all thoughts of me and the autocannon forgotten. Then I turned towards the big table near the center of the room, where all the heavy stick players hung out. They wore gold in their noses and ears, and no one ever, *ever* fucked with them. "I don't speak for Sammy," I explained, raising my voice so everyone in the place could hear. "No one speaks for Sammy but himself. If you've got any more shit-for-brains questions, why not come and ask them to my face?"

Suddenly The Warrens was filled with dead silence. Then Growly, the biggest stick player of them all, nodded slightly. As if the gesture were a command, the band struck up once again, the colored lights whirled and everything went on just as it always had.

Except from that moment forward I could feel Growly's eyes boring hard into the back of my neck. He didn't look away for an instant.

## Chapter Four

If Growly was gonna sit and drill eyeholes through me, I figured at least I ought to give him something interesting to look at. He was trying to intimidate me; the best way to counter was to dance like hell.

So I did. No one really knows why we anthro-rabbits so love to dance together, but the urge is almost universal. Sammy told me once he thought it might be because we were originally gengineered to assemble things in factories, and therefore the designers made us like to move together in a synchronized manner. Or maybe they'd reconfigured us to dance instead of craving continual physical contact with each other; real bunnies spend half their lives snuggled up into little balls together, and *that* wasn't any way to run a profitable business. It didn't matter to me; all I cared about was that it was Friday night, the Hop beat was grooving, and a good three dozen fellow bunnies were out on the dance floor formed up into regimented lines, shaking tail to the music.

Norms and felines and just about all the other sapient species that enjoy music tend to pair off in couples to dance, but we rabbits were wired differently. Like all other bunny-bucks I couldn't even get a hard-on unless a doe was putting out the right pheromones, and said does were gengineered in such a way that they wouldn't ever come into season unless they took special pills for a week ahead of time. That was to help keep the breeding programs on-track back in the days when we'd been owned, so throwbacks like Weiner, even if not culled outright, wouldn't ever sire or bear young. Does usually littered two or three offspring at a time and it was a hard pull indeed to simultaneously feed so many extra mouths in a place like the Zone, all the more so because most of us males tended not to give a shit about our kids. So does didn't drug-up very often, and as a result sex wasn't nearly as much an issue in our lives as it was for felines, canines, and perhaps especially norms. Therefore, we danced in large groups instead of pairs. The floor wasn't particularly crowded, so I choose a spot near the end of the front line where I could keep my back turned to Growly while still allowing him to watch me really, really close. I don't give a flying fuck what you think, my choice of floor space declared, and I'm not in the least bit scared of you, either. The band was playing "Hard Times", which was really popular just then, and I felt my body twist and writhe to the powerful beat.

"Hard times comin', you gotta be sure!
Hard times comin', find you the cure!"

Some of us bunnies prefer to dance choreographed steps, and the results can be quite impressive. But we mostly didn't dance to impress others, or at least I sure as fuck didn't. Instead I danced because I *had* to, because something inside was always straining to get out and I couldn't vent it any other way. Everyone else was doing a little hop every time the lyrics said "Hard"-- that part of the dance was communal, the part we needed each other for. A cream-colored doe with chocolate paws and ear tips danced next to me; she wore a printed t-shirt that said "Stew me!" on it. Her hips swayed easily to the song and she was snapping her head hard first to the left and then to the right on every second beat. I decided to elaborate and build on her pattern, stamping first one foot and then the other as she snapped her head. Meanwhile, on the other side of me a buck about my size wearing the gold finery of a successful stick dealer decided to stamp his feet too, but on the opposite beats. The dancers writhed, the music thumped along, colored lights swirled and flashed. Everything was shaping up splendidly. Then, right on cue, the beat sped up and the music intensified.

"Hard times suck but happen all'a time!
Hard times for ev'ryone till we all die!
Hard times laughin' at all that we try!
Hard times makin' us live lives of crime!"
That was more like it! As one, we danced harder and hopped higher.
"Hard times comin' to those who'd live free
Hard times promis'd to both you and me
Hard times livin' at the fuckin' norm's knee
Hard times all that anybody can see!"

22

I *liked* this song, I decided, as I poured my soul into the dance steps. My stamps became high kicks, my arm-motions angry punches, as all the while my midsection swayed back and forth with the powerful backbeat. All too soon, it was over.

"Hard times thrivin' inside every Zone
  Hard times growin' till the whole world blows!"

"Yeah!" I cried out at the last angry note of the song, just like every other bunny on the dance floor. We ended up turned every which way, but the next-door doe and I happened to be facing each other, arms in so close to the same positions we might almost have been looking into mirrors. She and I both ear-blushed, then looked away from each other.

"Yo!" a new voice interrupted me. It was Gash, Growly's number-one bag-man, who'd been waiting patiently for the music to end. Being a leopard, he wouldn't be caught dead dancing with us bunnies. "You got a minute? The set's over, and my boss wants to have a little talk-talk with you."

Sure enough, the band was shutting down for a break. I shook my head and sighed, then looked at the doe. "I'm just warming up," I complained.

She shrugged. "They played ten nonstop. What more can you ask? The rest of us are ready for a break, too." Then she smiled. "You're good."

I felt a little tingle somewhere inside of me; it represented, I was quite certain, a tiny fragment of normal romantic functionality that somehow the gengineers had missed. "I'm Gade," I explained, holding out a friendly hand for her to shake. "And you're pretty good yourself."

"I'm Fina," she answered, looking away. Her fur was warm and soft.

Then Gash cleared his throat. "It's not every day the Boss decides to apologize to someone," he pointed out.

"Alright already!" I protested, giving Fina's hand a little extra squeeze so as to drag out the moment a little longer. "Go tell Growly I'll be right there."

Fina's eyes widened at the mention of the tiger's name. "Growly?" she observed as Gash disappeared. "The big-time dealer? Growly's going to apologize? To you?"

I ear-blushed again. "I've got friends, is all..."

"Right," she agreed, pulling her hand back. Then her golden-brown eyes narrowed. "Sure. You've got friends." She rose up on her tiptoes and examined me with care. "Are you with the Avengers? Or maybe the West End Skullfuckers? I can't imagine who else Growly might apologize to. Where's your tattoos? And piercings?"

"Nowhere," I answered. "I'm not with any of them."

Her eyebrows rose, though clearly she didn't believe me. "Really?"

"Really," I assured her, looking deep into her eyes.

"Huh." she answered, looking confused. Then she smiled. "Well, you'd better be going. And I've got places I need to be myself. Do you come here often?"

"Every day," I assured her. "I live downstairs."

Her eyebrows rose again; not many bunnies could afford to live in such a classy place. "Well," she said slowly. "I'm new. And I expect I'll be around. Bye!"

# Chapter Five

It took me a long time to figure out why the big cats and even a few dogs hung out at The Warrens. They didn't particularly like the music, or at least not that I could tell, and their social structures weren't geared towards activities like group dancing. All they ever did was sit or lie around half-naked on heavily-upholstered lounge chairs and couches, hardly moving. When I was still little I'd thought they could just as easily have done that at home and saved the cover charge. Then I found out the big cats were originally gengineered as exotic sex toys and the whole thing came together for me. Especially once I also noticed it was almost always the cats who rented out the private rooms. They weren't just lying around; they were displaying themselves. And they did it at The Warrens because it was pretty much the only game in town. There simply weren't enough cats to support a nightclub of their own. Besides, what's the point of extreme vanity if there aren't any lesser beings around to look down upon?

Growly was getting a massage from a tigress when I finally arrived, the sort of slow, sensuous kneading only felines indulged in. The masseuse was collared, just like everyone had been back when we were slaves, and her jade-green pupils were the tiny pinpoints that marked a serious stick high. The cats sold sex as well as drugs and clearly this female was one of Growly's call girls - one of the more expensive ones, most likely. All big cats were beautiful. Even The Rope, a plain black jaguar, was drop-dead handsome in his dark, unadorned way. But the tigers, leopards, cheetahs and such, with their intricate markings and lean, super-athlete build... Fina, the doe I'd just been dancing with, was dumpy and pedestrian by any reasonable comparison. We rabbits had been bred to work, after all, not play. Not for the first time, I sighed and cursed my bad luck at having been born a rabbit instead of a privileged norm or sexy, virile cat. Growly didn't seem to notice me at first. But eventually, he purred and smiled. "Mmm! It's a rough life, but someone has to live it. Right?"

I smiled despite myself. Growly was a murderous drug-dealing bastard, but in his own way he had style. And a sense of pride as well, a trait shared by far too few others in the Zone. It was part of why I was more than a little afraid of him. "I guess," I replied, not committing myself.

"Sit down," he directed me, gesturing languidly. Instantly a chair appeared, and I did as I was told. "Care for a drink? Or perhaps a little something to touch yourself up?"

To be 'touched up' meant to be stuck. "No," I answered, crossing my arms defensively. "Not my bag."

"Smart kid," Growly observed. "We already knew that about you, though." Then the cat-man waved his hand again, and instantly the massage ceased. He rolled himself into a sitting position; it was like watching quicksilver flow. Then he smacked his lips a time or two and licked his nose. "Be a doll," he ordered his girl. "Leave us alone for a bit."

The collared masseuse sort of half-curtsied, then vanished back towards one of the private rooms. So did the rest of Growly's retinue. We sat in silence for a time, watching the band drift back towards the stage. I was just starting to grow uncomfortable with how things were dragging on when the tiger finally spoke.

"I'm sorry, kid," he began. "You were right to be pissed off at me for sending an old-time buddy to pump you." He shook his head sadly. "You deserve more respect than that."

If Growly expected an answer, I didn't know what it might be. Sammy claimed that in tough situations silence usually worked as well as anything, so I just sat and watched the drummer as he set himself up to play again.

Eventually, the tiger continued. "That was a world-class job you pulled off today, Gade. I don't know of anyone else who could've come close, even with the Wizard's help." The Wizard was Sammy. Only furs usually had nicknames; once again, Growly was trying to show respect by treating my mentor as if he were a true brother. The tiger reached down and picked up a glass of something that looked expensive, then raised it to me. "Salute!" I felt my ears darkening.

"It wasn't much," I answered, shrugging. "Not in the greater scheme of things."

Growly smiled, exposing his huge yellow fangs. "Maybe not much to *you*," he observed. "Because there's so many greater things still in store for you in the future. But from where a simple man of the street like me stands, it was a helluva thing."

I sighed and looked away. "Growly, you can save your line of shit for someone else. I honestly don't *know* why Sammy wanted an autocannon so bad, or what he's gonna use it for. That's the simple truth."

The tiger-man nodded, not taking offense. "He's a wily one, the Wizard. Hasta be or he'd have found an unpleasant end a very long time ago." Growly sipped at his drink. "But look at things from my point of view. A man in my position needs to know certain things." He met my eyes. "Like, who holds the heavy firepower."

I blinked, but said nothing.

"Order is a very important thing, Gade," Growly explained as if to a child. "Without order there can be no structured society. No one can work or buy or sell or even cash their welfare checks. And then where's an honest businessman like me?" He smiled, then nodded towards the rabbits who were lining up for the next dance. "Order is what makes civilized life possible, in the Zone or out. It's worth far more than gold. Or even than any one man's life."

"Sammy's not stupid," I answered eventually. "You just said that yourself." Then I lowered my ears and narrowed my eyes. "And he doesn't like being threatened, either."

"No, he's not stupid," Growly answered, smile gone. "Absofuckinglutely, he's not stupid." The tiger looked away and sighed, the sound a massive rumble in his huge chest. "It's the damnedest thing, how people tend to drop dead once the Wizard's taken a dislike to them. They get sick, strange accidents befall them, and sometimes they even get shot in the middle of the night when nobody can see shit. No, Sammy's not stupid." He sighed again. "This is why I'm taking such an interest here, Gade. I mean, if he doesn't want a war then why does he want that cannon so bad? If he does want a fight, then against who and why? My interests might be affected, you see. Or, if he just needs money..." Suddenly Growly was as cold as ice again. "I'll pay for that cannon, Gade. Pay a *lot*. More than anyone else can, just to preserve the social order for the good of everyone." His whiskers twitched, then he winked. "I'll even throw in a commission for you. My girl—the one that was just here? I saw how you were looking at her. Make this deal happen and you can have her all you want, whenever you want. Full- time, if it suits you." He leaned forward, bringing his face close to mine. "We can even make her smell right for you. You poor de-balled rabbit bastards! You don't know what you're missing!"

# Chapter Six

Sammy was already asleep when I got back home. I almost woke him up to let him know what Growly had said to me, but by the time I came staggering in he was snoring like hell. I'd stayed for two more dance sets just to send the tiger-man the message that what he thought about things wasn't all that important to Sammy and me, even if it wasn't quite true. Not looking scared, I'd learned young, was often half the battle. I didn't dance very well, though. No matter how hard I tried, I kept wondering what Sammy really *did* want the autocannon for. He wasn't in any way obliged to let me in on everything. It could well be that this was something he wanted to protect me from, even. But still...

Well, a guy just had to wonder.

The cannon was still set up on the main workbench. I had to pass within touching distance of the thing in order to get to my bedroom anyway, so it wasn't any big deal for me to rise up onto my toes and give it a good looking-over along the way. It was a rotary job, with six barrels and a big electric motor to keep the thing turning. Most automatics, like the stenguns Sammy made to sell to the gangs, tapped the power of the exploding powder charge to strip out the expended brass and feed a new cartridge. This meant that all the ammunition had to be of very nearly the same power and operate at the same pressure, or else the gun would jam. A rotary, however, could fire anything from blanks to armor-piercing rounds without missing a beat, in any mixture one cared to feed it. It was therefore far more versatile. The cannon had been armed with fifteen-millimeter general-purpose soft nose rounds when I stole it. The casings were long and evil-looking things, and I shuddered to imagine what the projectiles would've done to our getaway car if we'd given the beetle time to fire.

The reserve magazine contained tear gas rounds, tracers designed to scare the hell out of everyone in the neighborhood if fired at night, explosive rounds intended not to destroy things via their bursting charge but rather to transform themselves into harmless powder upon impact so they wouldn't hurt anything behind their target, and even a small clip full of armor-piercers that must have been included in the standard mix just in case we furs suddenly began pulling main battle tanks out of our asses. Sammy could never recreate the specialty rounds, I knew. Not with the tooling we had on hand. But already he'd turned out a very nice fifteen-millimeter brass cartridge case with a small primer-pocket to match the ones we used for the stengun ammo, and the CAD machine was loaded up with specs for a soft nose bullet to match. I picked up one of the armor-piercing rounds and pursed my lips. They looked simple enough to emulate as well, but in this case looks were deceiving. The anti-tank projectiles were sabot-fitted subcaliber rounds made of something very hard, and probably propelled to an ungodly velocity by a specialized propellant formula that'd taken a chemical engineer backed by a fully-equipped lab months to create. So, tempting though it might be to try, manufacturing more AP rounds was probably out of the question. Besides, it was hard to imagine what anyone might actually *need* such firepower for - in the Zone at least. The auto cannon could piss out soft-noses like water from a fire hose, which ought to be plenty good enough for anything Sammy and I might ever need to deal with. And more!

Which was exactly what was bothering me. Growly had got me to thinking, and I wasn't coming up with any good answers. I shook my head and sighed, then turned to the big gun rack on the wall. Sammy kept a fully-loaded stengun there at all times; just now there were four, his emergency standby plus three—he always made stens in sets of three to save time— ready for sale to pay our bills. The stens were crude, ugly things, and by no accident at all they always fell apart after a couple hundred rounds. All they were really good for was spraying general areas. Hanging just above the stens, however, were Sammy's real weapons, the pride and joy of a master machinist. He had a machine-pistol he wore under his coat that could group a dozen sten-rounds inside an inch at fifty yards, and a scoped automatic rifle that could do the same at a hundred. Deadliest of all was an antique big-game rifle fitted with a night-vision outfit. Sammy could kill a man-sized target nearly halfway across the Zone with the thing, or so he claimed, without anyone having more than the vaguest idea of where the shot might've come from. "So long as you only fire once," he'd explained to me back when I was learning to shoot, "they'll never locate you in time to do anything really dangerous." Not that this advice was of any immediate practical value to me; the weapon was so big and heavy I couldn't even hold it up to my shoulder. But soon after, Sammy'd built the auto-rifle. The infrared system also snapped onto it, and that gun fit me just fine...

Also hanging on the rack was an old zip-gun, the kind of thing Sammy sold when I was just little. It was made of pipe, used a nail for a firing pin, and was so primitive it didn't even look like a gun. You loaded the zip-gun by taking it apart, and fired it by banging on the nail with a rock or something. Back in the day, Sammy'd sold a crapload of the things. But then someone on the other end of the Zone had started making them too, and things got deadly for a while. Eventually Sammy won, but to do it he'd been forced to begin making and selling stens to the gangs who took up his side so they'd have an edge. After that he could never go back; his customers would never again settle for anything less than full-auto. Still, the zips were cool for booby-traps, all the more so because they looked like pieces of scrap-pipe. So we always kept one or two on hand to meet life's little challenges. I sighed and shook my head again. Sammy and I were, like, the best-armed pair in the whole fuckin' Zone and probably for a long way beyond it. We didn't need a fuckin' autocannon, or at least we didn't need one that I could see. Nor were we in terrible need of money, not from Growly or anyone else. So, why had I risked so much to get us one?

"*Sner-er-er-erk*," Sammy snored, half waking himself and then rolling over on his side. He had a plan, I knew. Sammy always had a plan, worked out twelve steps ahead and with every contingency considered. That was what made him so dangerous, I'd long since decided. Sure, the guns and poisons and shit helped. But it was his brain that made everyone else in the Zone tremble. In the end, that was why I kept on studying and shit. Because I could see how it paid off, in spades. And I was doing all right, I supposed.

But if I was so fucking smart, then why couldn't I figure out what we needed a goddamn cannon for?

# Chapter Seven

Saturday morning I almost went to the chinkshop. Sammy was no miser. He'd paid me very well indeed for my work the day before, so I had plenty to spend. And there was no doubting I wanted to get back to American Gangster. I'd killed Purvis before, yes, but never so quickly. Besides, he was an ugly fuck. Or in the game he was, at least. He stank too, even worse than Sammy did. Almost every young male fur I knew played American Gangster, and the one universal constant was how bad we all hated Melvin Purvis. He was every norm who'd ever cheated us, stole from us and fucked with our heads. But it was the very same norms who made the game and sold it to us for twice as much an hour as any other chinksession with less than a "XXX" rating.

I probably *would* have gone to the chinkshop, if I hadn't thought about how my fresh-earned money would end up right back in the norm's pockets just as surely as if I were patronizing a pawnbroker or buying stick or doing any of the other stupid shit that held us down in the Zone. The same stupid shit that left us too broke to leave, too dumb to do anything about it, and too fucked in the head to much care. But what else was there to do, besides hanging around, shooting the shit and drinking or drugging one's self into zombiedom?

Not much, I decided after standing outside The Warrens for a couple minutes, watching my breath make little puffs of mist in the cold air. A front had come through while I was sleeping, and it felt like it was going to snow. Back when I was little, snow had been cool. Sammy and I had made snowmen out in the alley, thrown snowballs at each other... He'd even made me a little sled and let me go racing down Ninth Street after an ice storm once, guarded every foot of the way by the eternally vigilant

Avengers. The sled was still in the storeroom somewhere...

Then I scowled, pulled my worn-out overcoat close around me, and turned towards Mrs. Rudder's Academy like I did every other goddamn Saturday morning of my life. It was lame, it was boring, and it was totally uncool. But what the hell else was there to do?

Mrs. Rudder ran her Academy out of the basement of the old Tenth Street Methodist Church building. It hadn't been a church in a very long time, but was still an impressive place regardless. The steeple was the highest point for blocks in all directions. This created an ideal vantage point for an Avenger lookout, and one was on duty there pretty much around the clock. Since they had to support the lookout post anyway, it was natural they should take over the rest of the building as well. The front of the place was the most heavily-tagged place in the Zone—there wasn't a square inch of surface area not plastered in arcane neon-hued symbology. And, of course, two guards shivered atop the stairs. "Gade," one of them greeted me respectfully as I climbed the steps. He was a feline, but not much bigger than me. His genome had been derived from domestic cat stock. "You the man!"

"Yeah!" the other agreed. He was a fellow rabbit, wearing sunglasses. But the lenses weren't so dark that I couldn't see he was stuck halfway out of his mind. "WayWayWay cool!" Then he held up his hand for me to slap in celebration. It was filthy, but I did it anyway. Then, I was inside.

The old church stank the way only a public building that never sees a mop anymore can. If anyone had scrubbed the toilets during my lifetime, it had to have been back before I learned to walk. The restrooms had clogged and clogged again, so many times the floors were buckled and warped from the continual soakings. But it wasn't just piss and shit that stunk the place up; even we furs needed to wash sometimes. Unfortunately, however, the Avengers weren't much on that sort of 'bullshit'. Most gang-bangers sprang from the most fractured and dysfunctional families in the Zone. Their parents hadn't washed or used civilized plumbing, so they didn't feel the lack even as the lice crawled through their fur and their teeth rotted out of their heads. The stick killed the discomfort, I supposed. As well as ensuring things didn't get too bad before the plug was finally pulled. It took years to thoroughly rot out a set of teeth, and stick was lethal enough that most users still didn't need dentures when they passed.

"Gade!" the Avengers greeted me as I eased my way up the center aisle between the old pews. Most were sleeping or, if not rabbits, screwing. But almost all the conscious ones waved and smiled as I passed. "My man!" "It's the Renegade!"

I smiled back but kept my hands firmly in my pockets. I didn't want to encourage any more high-fives. There were diseases present here that no doctor could cure.

Originally the building had been designed with many stairwells, but all of them had collapsed except one. This last holdout was directly behind the altar-curtain, a fact which I hated. The Avengers had many trophy-rooms and places of memory, but this was one of their largest. I wasn't by any means a god-fearing rabbit, yet what the gang-bangers had done to the once-holy place was... macabre. One wall was dedicated to the memory of departed comrades. Unlike more conventional memorials, however, this one was festooned with the weapons favored by the dead heroes—shivs, zip guns, chains, cruel-looking noodges, even a few axes still covered in dried gore. On the opposite wall was a similar setup, this one of trophies taken from the gang's enemies. And on the altar itself...

As I passed within five feet of the grisly display, I looked away. There, lined up in a neat row, were the severed heads of six Skullfucker sub-chieftains unlucky enough to find themselves on the losing end of a rumble. They'd been pickled or preserved somehow, but the stench was incredible regardless. This was due to a rather quaint Avenger custom. Since the toilets were all broken anyway, the head-display had become the communal urinal.

As always, or at least since I'd grown up enough to understand how fucked up it really was for the Zone's only school to be tucked directly underneath a desecrated church full of murderous substance-abusing psychopaths, I clenched my fists in rage and descended the steps to the Academy. It wasn't Mrs. Rudder's fault; there weren't a lot of places in the Zone where a bunch of kids could be kept relatively safe from about a billion different kinds of predators, and even fewer where the rent was low enough for her to be able to pay it. Not that she could swing it on her own; Sammy's fingerprints could be found all over the operation, if one knew where to look. The water still worked in this part of the building, for example, and the Avengers never, ever came downstairs, no matter what. Besides, Sammy and Mrs. Rudder were a little sweet on each other. Sometimes she came over to our place and I had to go dance for a while.

About halfway down the stairs the whole atmosphere of the place changed. A huge fan at the bottom was kept always turned on, which held most of the stink at bay. All by itself, that helped a lot. But the paint was also fresh and bright, the floor was clean, and there weren't piles of used-up sticks lying around all over the place.

"Why, Simeon!" Mrs. Rudder greeted me as I rounded the corner and entered her classroom. "What a pleasant surprise! Sam told me not to expect you today."

*He don't know shit*, I started to say. But beyond Mrs. Rudder, all clustered together around a single computer terminal, were about a dozen of the richest, luckiest, cleanest, and healthiest children in the Zone. I'd once been one of said kids myself, and still felt kind of funny cursing in the presence of my old primary-school teacher. "I do have the weekend off," I explained more formally. "But..."

Mrs. Rudder sort of glowed. "Wonderful!" she repeated. "We were just getting ready to enjoy a story together. Would you like to read for us?"

"Yay!" the kids cried out together, swarming over me like a soft, furry wave. They all loved me to death, though I never quite understood why. Perhaps because I was the only non-norm they'd ever met who already knew the stuff they were struggling to learn and was willing to help them with it instead of laughing in their faces and calling them ugly names and stealing their backpacks?

We read for a couple hours, swapping books around as necessary to allow for the missing pages so that everyone got to try and read everything. Then we did math, played a dodge-ball game I had to work very hard at losing, and the school day was over. Mrs. Rudder only taught for a half-day on Friday and Saturday because the streets got bad early on the weekends. The Avengers might be on the lookout, but even they could only do so much. Every year or two Mrs. Rudder would lose a student. When that happened class would be cancelled for about a week while she disappeared – to where no one knew - to mourn in private. Then she'd emerge haggard, drawn and empty and resume her hopeless attempt to water the endless Sahara of the Zone with the leaky soup-can of her pathetic little school, another piece of her heart gone forever.

"Thank you so much," Mrs. Rudder said to me as we cleaned up after class. I was feeding Chucky the Fifth, the class pet. He was a white rat, and far cleaner about his person than most of the furs who lived upstairs. Most animals were, I suspected. Once upon a time I'd earned the right to feed Chucky the Second by getting a hundred-percent on a spelling test, and ever since I'd still considered it to be my personal privilege.

"Not so much fruit!" Mrs. Rudder complained, like she always did. "You'll spoil him!" But, again like always, she indulged me. I was one of her very first Zone students, and the only graduate not already on stick, in jail, chilled, or working a brainless, menial, soul-killer of a dead-end job.

"Sorry," I answered, not really meaning it.

"It's all right." She sighed, and then smiled as Chucky chittered merrily over his Saturday feast. "At least someone in this hellhole is happy."

I shook my head, but said nothing. Eventually, Mrs. Rudder spoke again. "I know about the autocannon, Simeon," she said. "I can't say that I approve, mind you. But I understand. And I'm glad you're safe."

I looked away, feeling something I hadn't known was hurting ease up a little inside of me. "Thank you."

She shook her head. "If only..." Then she sighed again and began turning out the Academy's lights. "But there's no point wishing for that which can never be, is there? You'd think I'd eventually learn." Then she headed off to the back room for her coat. "Don't leave yet, dear. I'd appreciate if you walked me out to the street. One day a week, at least, I'm not afraid."

## Chapter Eight

Mrs. Rudder had an apartment in one of the big buildings over on Walnut, where a lot of the working furs lived. Like Sammy, she was the only norm in her building. But unlike him, she didn't live in a fortress. What kept her alive, I could only imagine. I didn't have anything else to do, so I walked her all the way home. Duane Generalservices met us at the door and smiled at me, his long fangs standing out against the dark Rottweiler fur of his face. Duane was Mrs. Rudder's security guard, most Saturdays. He'd tried to learn to read, my former teacher had told me once, but between the three jobs he worked to keep his family under a decent roof, he just hadn't been able to make time. Duane didn't like me very much, probably because I carried myself like an outlaw and had a bad reputation in certain circles. But he'd also known my parents and taken note of how much Mrs. Rudder thought of me. So, his smile was genuine if guarded as he held the door open for his sole norm resident. "Hi, Gade! What's up?"

"Not much," I allowed, smiling back as best I was able. Duane Generalservices was in my mind representative of a whole class of furs that left me deeply conflicted inside. On the one hand, they were good and decent folks doing their best to raise their families under impossible conditions. Yet they were also ball-less sheep, bowing and scraping to the norms every chance they got in exchange for whatever crumbs they might be thrown. Duane hadn't even bothered to change his name after the June Revolution; he still carried that of his one-time corporate owner. My parents, by contrast, had chosen a new surname from among the finest and boldest in the history books and then named me after its greatest scion. Thus, I was Simeon Bolivar, not Simeon Clevelandlaborsolutions as most certainly would have been the case had Duane been my father. And how fucked up would my head have been *then*?

With Mrs. Rudder safely back at home, I found myself at loose ends again. I scowled to myself as I walked down Walnut, carefully noting and nodding to each Avenger lookout as I passed by. Sammy made me read three news-sites a week; one of these was geared to norm teens. As near as I could tell from the fucked-up thing, the biggest problem norm kids my age had was too much time on their hands. They filled the empty hours with dances, all kinds of nitpicky talk about music, and most of all trying to decide which kind of expensive shit to rub on their faces. Maybe their faces really did need to have expensive shit rubbed on them; acne looked *painful*. So that part, at least, I didn't hold against them. But still... How much bitching about school did Sammy expect me to read about, when their classrooms weren't hidden under gang-houses and their textbooks weren't missing about a dozen pages each? How long did Sammy expect me, an orphan, to listen to the norm kids complain about how their parents didn't buy them the right gifts or let them go to the right parties? And how many pictures did he expect me to look at of spacious, pretty houses maintained by fur gardeners and fur maids, when he and I lived in a fallout shelter under a noisy nightclub with automated machine guns—even worse, automated machine guns we actually *needed!*-- for a security system? Sometimes, especially on Saturdays after school let out for the little ones, it was just too fucking much. Bitch, bitch, bitch all the time, when they lived in fucking heaven!

"What did you just say?" a voice suddenly demanded.

I was startled out of my reverie. "Huh?" I demanded intelligently, swinging around to face whoever had snuck up behind me. Inside my jacket pocket, my fingers sought the special hide-out pistol Sammy had made for me.

But it wasn't necessary. "I was just wondering what you were muttering about, with your face all sour," a familiar doe replied, speeding up her pace a little so we could walk side-by-side. It was tubby little Fina, who I'd danced with at The Warrens. "I saw you walking Mrs. Rudder to her apartment, so I figured I'd come out and say hello." Her head tilted a little to one side. "How come you know her?"

I smiled a little. Should I tell Fina my mentor was shagging her? Somehow, it didn't seem quite the right approach. "She used to be my teacher," I explained. "I still help her out on Saturdays sometimes."

"Wow!" the girl-bunny replied, her eyes widening a bit. "That is *so* cool! But..." Then she stopped in her tracks so suddenly I took another full step before I could react. "You can't be," she declared.

I felt my eyebrows rise. "Can't be who?"

"Can't be the same Simeon Mrs. Rudder is always going on about 'So smart', she says one minute, and then 'so good with the little ones' the next." She shook her head. "But, you're a *criminal*!"

I laughed, and then rocked my head slightly from side to side as I thought about how to answer. "Maybe," I replied. "The criminal part, I mean. That's a definite maybe, in fact. But I have to admit it. I'm also Simeon."

Fina's reaction surprised me. Her brows lowered, her back straightened, her hands formed fists, and suddenly she was mad as hell at me. "Ooo-*oh*!" she complained, putting said fists on her hips. "If only I'd known!"

By now I was getting a little angry myself. Sammy was always cracking wise about how unpredictable the females of all species were; now, for the first time I was beginning to understand it wasn't just a dumb joke. "What?" I demanded. "I mean..."

"*Oooh*!" she repeated in a near-snarl. Then the storm was past as if it had never been, and the bunny-girl was walking alongside me again. "I work at the school Monday through Friday," Fina explained eventually. "I've only been on the job for two weeks. Saturdays I help out my sister. She's got three little bunnies in diapers. And on Sundays, Mrs. Rudder is teaching me to read."

I nodded slowly. "It's a good thing to know," I agreed. Then I quoted Sammy. "There's so much more out there, than... This."

"So I'm starting to figure out," Fina agreed. When I turned to face her she was staring at me. "Mrs. Rudder says you're the best student she ever had, period. And she used to teach norms."

"Really?" The last part, at least, was news to me. I felt my ears blushing. It was uncomfortable in the cold. "I don't think I'm all that smart. Without Sammy's help, I'd be just another pincushion."

"And without my parents, so would I," the doe replied. "We both owe so much to others."

Suddenly, I was angry again. Though I wasn't sure quite why. "Our whole world is shit," I declared, apropos of nothing. "We live out our shitty little lives in a shitty little shithole of a neighborhood. We can dream of breaking out of here, but no one ever really does. Not any of us furs, at least."

Fina shrugged. "There's a few Outside," she countered.

"Pampered pets. Still living as slaves, though their chains have been cut for years now." I scowled again.

"Not slaves," Fina countered. "Servants. And performers."

"Slaves in my book." I stopped and sighed, then shook my head. "Sorry. I'm having a bad day. Seeing those beautiful little kids trying to learn in a place like that..."

"I know," the pudgy doe replied. She was looking at me again, and in some mysterious way her eyes seemed to be penetrating deep inside me. "It's a messed-up world. Ugly enough to spoil anyone's outlook on life."

"Fuckin' A," I agreed. Then I realized that somehow we'd walked two whole blocks together and I hadn't noticed. "Listen, this is Saturday. It can get pretty nasty hereabouts..."

"Right," Fina agreed, nodding. She had a scar on her face, I realized suddenly. Not a terrible one; her fur nearly concealed it. The wound ran upwards from the left corner of her mouth almost all the way to her eye. Something had laid her open in a very serious way at one time or another. Yet she didn't seem to let it bother her much. "I don't even go to The Warrens on Saturday nights, much less down *this* street." Her right arm jerked, as if she'd almost reached out to touch me and then changed her mind. "Even for a guy, it's rough. Are you sure you'll be all right?"

I smiled. "There isn't a street in the Zone I can't walk down, though it's not because I'm especially tough. Sure, on some of them I might have to answer a few questions or explain myself. But nobody fucks with me in a serious way." I let my grin widen. "I have friends, like I said last night."

Fina looked away. Clearly, as a general rule she didn't approve of that sort of friend. "Well... In that case I'll be heading home now. Sis'll be wondering where I'm off to." She smiled a little. "See you around, Simeon."

"See you!" I answered reflexively, though I should've asked her to call me Gade. People would laugh at me if she ever did that out in front of anyone. Then I stood and watched her as, hands thrust deep into her jacket pockets, Fina turned and headed back towards her home. She was fat, very much overweight, even. Her legs were short by bunny standards, and her face was plain. But her scent was sweet and pure.

I stood and watched her every second until she turned the corner and vanished from sight.

# Chapter Nine

Chestnut Street was one of the most violent places in the entire Zone. Oddly enough, this was the direct result of a truce that'd been declared there years back, so that no single gang controlled Chestnut between Eighth and Eleventh. The only genuine supermarket in the Zone was located at Ninth and Chestnut. While a few other little grocers were still in business here and there, a lot of the more specialized-diet types couldn't survive without the market. In the early days Joe's Superama had been the focus of one bloody battle after another, until the violence grew so bad Joe shut the place down entirely for two weeks to sort of make a point. Since the major gang leaders at the time had all been of the feline persuasion, and since Joe's was the only place selling stuff palatable to cats, the wars had ended almost overnight. Since then the Avengers' territory had steadily grown, largely due to their close association with Sammy, so Chestnut Street formed a sort of deep salient into their holdings. If the wars ever started again I reckoned the Avengers could probably seize and hold the area, if they really tried. But it'd cost lotsa blood, so much that as yet they hadn't made their move. I wondered how long it'd be.

No one had much interest in policing ground not producing revenue and the Chestnut district was no exception. There were muggers, rapists, and every other kind of two-bit sleazebag aplenty to be found anywhere one might go in the Zone, but it was only near Joe's that they operated with impunity, in no fear whatsoever of retaliation from the gangs. Or almost no fear; there were a few ground rules everyone understood. If you fucked with a connected man, for example, you could expect to be fucked with in return—most likely fatally. Friends were friends and blood was blood, even on Chestnut Street. The only people I really had to worry about were either dumbshits too stupid to know who I was, or else a total nutcase. Once, a nutcase had mugged me. His corpse was found hanging upside down from a lamppost the next morning with a nail driven into the braincase: a Skullfuckers' trademark kill. Just in case anyone didn't get the point, a note was pasted to the mugger's chest. It read "Our respects to Sammy and Gade." The very next day my wallet and knife arrived back home, carried through Avenger lines by a heavily escorted Skullfucker courier.

I was still pretty much at loose ends and had just decided to duck into Joe's for something fresh and green when a black-and-white clad rabbit fell in alongside me. Black and white were Skullfucker colors. But I didn't need the hint. Shiv had once attended school with me. He'd been pretty smart, too; bright enough to already be a sub-chieftain. "Gade!" he said, sidling in easily alongside me. Two lampposts away I saw an Avenger bunny scowling at us. The Avengers didn't like it when either Sammy or I had dealings with the Skullfuckers. But what could they do about it?

"Shiv," I acknowledged my one-time classmate. Once upon a time we'd read The Jungle Books and many other happy tales together. He'd even visited me a time or two at home, something Sammy never let anyone else do. But things had changed since then, in a very serious way. In order to become a Skullfucker sub-chieftain, one had first to kill an enemy in fair fight and then another slowly. Mrs. Rudder and I spoke often of her previous students, but neither of us ever, ever mentioned Shiv. "How're they hangin'?"

He held his hand out to be slapped, and out of politeness I did so. Shiv wasn't as dirty as most gang-bangers. In fact, he was nearly as clean and well-dressed as I was. Nor could I detect any sign of stick about him. This didn't surprise me; he'd always been one of the brightest. "Real good, Gade," he answered, grinning and putting a little extra swagger into his step as we passed the Avenger. Other than that they ignored each other totally, as Chestnut Street protocol dictated. He smiled, exposing file-pointed incisors. "I'm making a real name for myself."

"Heh!" I agreed noncommittally, turning away. Filed teeth were common enough, but it made my head hurt just to look at the nasty things. They weren't natural, somehow.

"You done good yesterday!" Shiv continued, deliberately bumping into me - a cool way to, like, slap someone on the back. "Jesus fucking Christ almighty, Gade! That took brains and balls both."

I shrugged. It was easy to guess what was coming next. "And you want to know what Sammy's going to do with the auto cannon."

Shiv shrugged. "It'd be nice, I admit. But I ain't that stupid, Gade. I know you better than that." He deliberately bumped into me again. "You and me, we're the smartest motherfuckers in the whole fuckin' Zone. Except for Sammy."

"And Mrs. Rudder," I pointed out.

"Cunts don't count." Shiv looked away and scowled, suddenly angry about something. But in an instant it passed. "So when Zoomo asked me to find out what the fuck, I told him up front you weren't gonna talk." He shrugged. "So, I'm just here to send Zoomo's regards and visit with an old friend."

I looked down at my feet for a time, thinking over my reply. Zoomo was the top Skullfucker, and had been for almost two years. That was a record. "Well," I said eventually. "Please return my greetings to Zoomo. And tell him that so far as I know there aren't any outstanding grudges."

"So far as you know." Shiv's, eyes narrowed.

"So far as I know," I repeated, shrugging. "Shit, Shiv! You've met Sammy. Do you think he tells me every fuckin' little detail?"

"Nope," my one-time friend replied, looking off into the distance. "That's part of what makes him such a dangerous motherfucker." He turned back to face me. "You know," he said softly. "We got along real good when we were little. When you were Simeon, and I was Jeffrey."

"We did," I agreed, refusing eye-contact.

"It's kinda sad how we've drifted apart." Shiv sighed, and then shook his head. "I'm movin' up fast, Gade. As fast as anyone ever has."

"Yeah." It was a flat, noncommittal monosyllable.

"Did you ever wonder?" he asked after an awkward silence. "I mean... You're *bitchin'*, Gade! The only other fuckin' rabbit I really respect. You and I, we could..."

"Run the entire Zone together?" I asked gently. "With an autocannon to back us, of course."

He met my eyes again. "Like I said, you ain't dumb."

I sighed, then lowered my head and began walking again. "Shiv, don't take this wrong, okay? I don't mean any disrespect. But for us to do that, you'd hafta waste Zoomo and I'd hafta... do the same to Sammy." I choked a little on the last part; the words didn't want to come out. "That's what you're suggesting. Isn't it?"

Shiv smiled a sad smile. "Everyone dies, Gade. It ain't no big deal."

"Maybe not," I answered, turning away. "But I just couldn't do it, Shiv. Chill Sammy, that is. Not for the whole Zone. Not even for a whole universe of Zones."

Shiv smiled again. "I expected that," he answered. "And no disrespect is taken." His expression faded. "But he's gonna die someday, Gade, even if no one offs him. He's old. You know it and I know it. So all I'm saying is, maybe you oughta be giving a little thought to your future. About how you're gonna survive without the Wizard's magic to protect you." He smiled again. "Take your time, friend Renegade. When the day comes, not only will I be there for you but so will the Skullfuckers. I promise."

## Chapter Ten

I ended up not getting any fresh greens after all. Once Shiv was done with me I felt sick and cold inside; not at all in the mood for a treat. It was always like that when I talked to an old friend who'd fallen from grace. But this was worse somehow, because Shiv was right. I wasn't stupid. And Sammy *would* die someday, no matter what I did. Where the fuck would I be then?

I was feeling low indeed as I re-entered Avenger territory and nodded my respects to Doolie, who was back on watch again. The whole world was fucked up, near as I could tell, maybe even more fucked up than it'd been back when Mom, Dad and Sammy had engineered the local Uprising together. At least then we furs hadn't spent half our time wasting each other. We hadn't been filthy and diseased and greedy and allowed so much stick that we rotted our own brains out, either. Sure, we'd been owned, exploited, worked half to death, not permitted even to choose our own mates...

But at least we hadn't had to worry about how the fuck we were still supposed be alive five years from now!

I was hoping Sammy might be at home and working on something when I got back to our little hidey-hole. He didn't mind talking while he was working on shit; in fact, it was the best time to hold a conversation with him. He was always happy when making or fixing something, happy in a way that I sort of envied him. For all the hours I spent with him on the lathe, the drill press and the tridee alloy printer I was still only a fraction as good with my hands as my mentor was, and both of us had long since come to appreciate I'd never be his equal. I was reasonably competent; he was a fuckin' mechanical genius. It might've been easier to take except that no fur had ever proven to be exceptionally gifted with tools, according to my books. Sammy'd done his best for me, but even he knew that he'd met with only limited success. Apparently, such advanced levels of tool-using skills simply weren't in our genes. No matter how many Uprisings there were and how many hours we spent in training, we'd never be Wizards. Never, in this one area at least, be the equals of the norms.

Just like I was beginning to suspect we'd never be competent to run our own society, either. Maybe we were better off being owned...

There were no less than eight Avengers standing outside The Warrens when I rounded the last corner on my way home. The biggest, baddest Avengers there were, in fact. All were of carnivorous stock, and all wore coats with bulges about the size of stenguns under them. Stonecold's bodyguard, for certain.

I shook my head and thrust my hands deeper into my pockets as I approached the entrance to the nightclub. It wasn't dark yet, and normally The Warrens would still be pretty much deserted. But there stood The Rope, watching the door much earlier than usual. Which made sense, I supposed. Stonecold was Chief of the Avengers, which made him one of the biggest VIP's in the Zone and the target of god-only-knew how many assassination plots at any given moment. He didn't leave his lair often, mostly for this reason, and god help whoever had the miserable luck to own the building the Chief of the Avengers got whacked in. His successor would make it his first order of business to waste him, along with everyone else who just might maybe've had anything to do with the regicide. It was after all the prudent thing to do. Even if said successor was the one who'd arranged the hit in the first place. Perhaps especially so, in that case.

The Rope wasn't nearly as cheerful as usual, being surrounded by the most notoriously trigger-happy of all the Avengers. I decided to simply keep my cool and act like nothing major was going down. "Heya, Rope!" I greeted my friend as I walked up the three concrete steps and across the broad patch of sidewalk separating The Warrens from the street.

"Gade!" he greeted me in return, smiling a little despite his nervousness.

"How's it going?" I asked the Bengal tiger-morph who was clearly the leader of Stone's bodyguard. "Is everything cool?"

His eyes narrowed a little, but apparently he had his orders. "For you, they're cool," he rumbled, stepping aside just enough for me to edge past him and through the door. "For now."

I smiled back, employing my best dopey-harmless-bunny smile. Avenger bodyguards were institutionally paranoid, and about as macho as macho got. They made it a point never to employ a pleasant word when an implied threat would serve equally well. So I didn't take it personally.

Two and two had come together for me almost from the moment I'd realized who the bodyguards were. Therefore, I wasn't at all surprised to find another pair of Avengers halfway down the little hallway leading to my home. They had their orders too; as I approached they stood a little straighter and reached under their coats. My own hands had long since left my pockets; I kept them well away from my sides as I eased my way down the corridor. "Heya!" I greeted them, still smiling my dopey-smile. "I'm just trying to go home, guys."

"Stop right there, Gade," one of them directed. "You're carrying, and we know it. It ain't personal and there's no outstanding grudge. But we've got orders."

I smiled a little wider. If Stone was downstairs chatting with Sammy in his innermost lair, as I figured just about had to be the case, then my little handgun was about the *last* thing his bodyguards should've been worried about. My mentor could hold off a fuckin' army down there, and that was *before* he'd scored the auto cannon. Stone was a fly trapped in a technological spider web, guards or no, and he'd leave alive only by my mentor's sufferance. But there wasn't any point rubbing it in. So instead of bitching, I just nodded. "Right," I agreed, sounding as reasonable as possible. Then, moving very slowly, I pulled a little data pad out of my pants pocket. "I've got homework to do," I explained. "Would you mind if I sat here to do it?"

The guards looked at each other, and then one of them shrugged. "Fuck if I care. Just don't do anything stupid."

I smiled again. Despite all their protests to the contrary, reading and writing were a little magical to the average gang-banger. Mysterious, in other words, and interesting. The fact was, they wanted to watch. So I sort of slid my back down the wall, turned on my pad...

...and pressed my head firm up against the heater vent, so my sensitive ears could pick up every word of the 'secret' discussion going on down below.

# Chapter Eleven

"...here you are rattling on about elections and governments and shit again," Stone was complaining as I settled in and turned on my screen. One of my defaults was to the New York Times; I chose it to impress the guards since there were usually both pictures and a lot of fine print. They wouldn't notice I wasn't actually turning pages. They probably weren't even aware that I was supposed to. "Ain't you learned nothin', Wizard? I was around for the Uprising too, you know. That shit just don't fly."

A long pause ensued. In my mind's eye it was easy to picture gray-bearded Sammy looking off into the distance, the way he always did when he was really thinking about something. "It's *got* to fly," he answered eventually. "Look, Stone. For almost fifteen years now the norms have held off. They've let us try and work this shit out on our own, because they figured that all they could do by sticking their noses into our business was fuck things up even worse. "

"They're goddamn right about that!" a new voice interjected. It was Growly, the drug dealer. What was *he* doing down there?

"It's what's always happened before to us norms, you see, whenever we've tried to fix societies we weren't actually part of. In fact history is mostly a series of..." His voice trailed off, and then he sighed. What did Growly and Stonecold understand of history? "Anyway, it just doesn't work when we try to fix things up for people, instead of helping them help themselves. Besides, the norms Outside know they fucked up royally by making you guys slaves to begin with. They feel bad about it, even today. So they've been patient."

"They charge us taxes," Stonecold complained.

"Only for earnings outside the Zone," Sammy countered. "Inside, we've got full autonomy. That was the deal, for every Zone in the world.

But it was only supposed to be a first step. We were supposed to elect leaders, you see. Form a government. Pass laws that suited the unique needs of our culture. Build our own schools, police our own streets. All that shit."

"We *did* elect people," Growly pointed out. "Hell, I campaigned for the Bolivars myself. Donated money, even though back then I was just a small-time nobody. But they got whacked the first time they tried to enforce a law that pissed someone off."

A law that pissed *you* off, I didn't say aloud. My mother and father had tried to outlaw or at least regulate stick. And, they'd died for it. Just like all the leaders in all the other Zones had either died or turned into crimelords themselves.

"And we never held another election," Sammy agreed. "Because we couldn't. The Provisional Police broke up into armed mobs, then unarmed mobs when the ammo ran out. You were one of them, Stone. It was all clubs and knives there, for a while." Sammy sighed again. "Ah, the good old days..."

"Heh," Stonecold snorted. "Then you turned as rotten as any of the rest of us, Wizard. Maybe even rottener." His tone turned icy. "You picked and chose who got the best guns, and charged us every cent we could possibly pay for them."

"So I'm not entitled to a living?" Sammy demanded, his voice hardening. "What the fuck is *this*, Stone? It's not like you haven't made out pretty goddamned well, considering. Or you either, Growl. You want to try and manufacture your own fucking guns?"

"Easy there, Wizard," Growly interjected, his voice warm and reasonable. "You've got our full respect, mine and Stone's both." I could imagine the gang leader and the big drug-dealing lion exchanging an icy glare. "You had to help keep order. There has to be order, after all. I was just explaining that to Gade last night, when I was congratulating him on his take. Helluva kid, he is. His parents'd be proud."

"You stay the hell away from Simeon," Sammy growled. "Both of you. That's part of our standing deal."

"Whatever," Growly replied. "I was just trying to show my respect, was all." He sighed. "Wizard, you can't protect him forever. You gotta know that. He's bright, sharp, and able as hell. I could offer him a real future, if you'd let me."

"Me too," Stone added. "I'd give him a squad from day one, just for what he pulled off yesterday alone. Maybe even a platoon." His voice darkened again. "One of his best friends is a Skull, though."

"You stay the fuck away," Sammy repeated, though less angrily this time. "And let *me* worry about his future. Not that there's going to be much of a future for any of us if we don't get our shit together here. Like I said, the norms won't wait forever."

"So what're they going to do?" Growly demanded. "Try and police the Zone, with every fur hating them more than anything in the universe? I still remember some tricks from the Uprising, by God! It'd never work."

"Anything they did would just make us hate them that much more," Stone agreed. "Last time, we won. If they want a rematch, we'll just have to fuck 'em again. Right up the ass!"

Sammy sighed. "It's not that simple. We don't live in a vacuum, here. There's all kinds of shit you haven't considered."

"Like?" Growly snapped.

"Disease, for one," Sammy explained. "You guys are part-human, and some of the shit you get sick with can spread to norms. The sewer systems are about shot. In some places, they already *are* shot. We're fucking up the norm's water, in a very dangerous way."

"How so?" Stone demanded. "What's us being sick got to do with anyone else?"

A long, long silence followed. "It matters," Sammy said eventually. "Trust me. It matters a lot, and the norms know it. Then there's the crime outside the Zone. The norms don't like the stick trade. It's illegal to even make the shit these days. But furs pay so high for it that some people see the risk as worth taking anyway. Your suppliers, Growly..."

"Business is fucking business," the lion countered.

"They're getting so rich they're buying the judges and corrupting the whole society. You think *you're* in the money? You oughta see *their* bank balances! Norms don't like having their judges bought and sold, Growly. They don't care for it at all. And then there's the other crime all around the Zone, the break-ins and burglaries and such. We're dragging property values down all around us-- every Zone in the world is. The total cost is probably in the tens of billions. Enough, I'd say, that eventually some norm's going to decide it's time to do something about it. Sooner more likely than later."

"Shit!" Stone objected. "First you send Gade out to jack a gun from the pigs of all people, and then you bitch about too much Outside crime! Ain't *that* a motherfucker?"

"You're talking out of both sides of your mouth, Wizard," Growly agreed.

"Maybe," Sammy agreed. "But I need that cannon."

"Why?" Growly demanded, his voice filled with anguish. "What in the name of god *for*?"

"To make the elections happen," he explained patiently.

"But..." the lion-man objected. "I mean..."

"We don't want no fuckin' elections!" Stone protested. "They'd fuck *everything* up!"

"How unfortunate," Sammy observed. "How terribly unfortunate indeed."

# Chapter Twelve

I wouldn't have thought that jack-shit was wrong, if all I'd had to go by was Growly's and Stonecold's departure. Or at least I wouldn't have until I made it downstairs. The two Zone crime lords seemed even more pleased than usual to see me. Growly asked me to read a few lines from the Times aloud to him, and then he and Stone laughed and patted me on the head as if I were only half my true age. "You keep that shit up," Growly directed, nodding at my data pad. "It'll pay off for you someday."

Sammy wasn't in nearly such a good mood. He was mad as hell, though clearly not at me. When I came through the door he was drinking a cup of coffee and glaring down at his workbench, where the single prototype auto cannon shell he'd completed sat waiting to be tested.

"Hi," I greeted him, knowing better than to say much more. When Sammy was glaring, as a rule it was best not to bother him.

But this time was an exception. "Hi, yourself!" he greeted me, forcing a smile. Sammy looked very tired, I realized suddenly. The lines on his face were a lot deeper than they'd been when I was little. And his eyes seemed almost to have a film over them. "Whatcha been up to?"

I shrugged, then went to the refrigerator and poured myself some juice. Sammy didn't like juice; he bought the stuff just for me. "Nothing much, really. I helped out at the school a little bit."

My mentor's face brightened a little. "How's Alice?"

"Good. I walked her home." Then I shrugged again. "Other than that, not much." I looked Sammy in the eye. "Though, everyone and their brother wants to know what the fuck about your new toy."

Sammy smiled. It made him look a little better, though the lines were still plenty deep. "Ain't that the truth?" He sipped a little coffee before speaking again, then picked up his prototype shell and toyed with it absently. "That's what Growly and Stone were just here about."

I nodded. "Growly asked me about it last night. I almost woke you up to tell you."

"You should have," Sammy corrected me. "Though it's not any big deal."

I shrugged. "And Shiv hit me up about it today, on behalf of the Skulls."

"They *would* send Jeffrey to see you," Sammy agreed, looking off into the distance.

I pressed my lips together, deciding whether or not to say any more. Then, I realized I *had* to. Sammy needed to know this kind of shit, to help keep us both alive. "He figures that us two could take over the whole Zone with that cannon. If we wasted you and Zoomo, that is."

"Ha!" Sammy replied, slapping his knee. "I *knew* it! Even way back when." Suddenly he was grinning like a little boy. Then his expression faded and he looked deep into my eyes. "*Could* you, Simeon? Theoretically, I mean. After all, I reckon that if you were actually going to do me, you wouldn't have given me any warning."

I smiled back, and then looked off into the distance to think. "Maybe," I allowed. "It'd take some planning."

His eyes narrowed, like they always did when he was serious about something. "How?"

"Well... I can run the machines, right? But I'm still not you. So I'd have to time things carefully. You're the one who always scores the raw materials-- I don't know where or how you get them. I'd have to chill you when we've got plenty of stengun makings in stock, and worry about making new connections later."

"Right," he agreed, nodding.

"Then..." I paused and thought some more. "The Skulls aren't nearly as strong as the Avengers. I'd have to fix that, probably even before Shiv wasted Zoomo. The best way to do it would be to hook them up with all the minor outfits." I wriggled my nose furiously.

"Good," Sammy continued, nodding again.

"To make that happen... Well, the only way I can think of would be for the Avengers to threaten them somehow. Threaten them hard, in a way no one else could tolerate. Also, that way the Skulls and whoever would have to immediately rally behind a new leader when Zoomo met with his accident. They wouldn't have the time or space to fuck around with internal power struggles. It'd be mostly up to Shiv to see that he became the leader in question. I dunno much about Skull politics, but my money'd be on him. He's smart, all right."

Sammy shook his head. "Damn, kid! You're growing up." He smiled again. "Go on. I'm utterly fascinated."

"So," I continued. "That's the tipping point. I'd have to see to it that the Avengers got fucked somehow, right at the critical moment. Bad ammo, maybe. Or more likely make 'em all gather together in one place and hose 'em down with the cannon. That's one deadly motherfucker, I'd imagine." I shook my head sadly. "Jesus! It'd fuckin' *slaughter* them! We could hunt down the rest and kill them one by one after that, whenever we liked."

"That'd be that," Sammy agreed, looking at me strangely. "You and Jeffrey running it all, and probably no one else with enough balls to take the two of you on for twenty, maybe even thirty years after such a bloodbath. People don't forget shit on that sort of scale very quick."

I shrugged again, and then sipped at my juice. "It's just like planning out a job," I explained. "Except I'd never... I mean..." I'm not sure just how it happened, but suddenly Sammy and I were hugging like I was a little kid again. And I was crying, too. Both of us were.

"I know," Sammy answered; his voice soft and calm. "I know." A long, warm silence developed, and then Sammy spoke again. "I'm *so* proud of you, Simeon. You've worked hard, grown up straight and tall, and fulfilled every last one of my hopes and dreams for you. You're tough, smart and strong, exactly what's needed here and now." He pulled away and looked into my eyes again. "And just a wee bit ruthless, as well. Which is all to the good in someone like you." His smile grew very cold, despite the tears.

"It's what your parents lacked, you see."

# Chapter Thirteen

Theoretically I had Sunday off, too. But I didn't feel much like doing anything. Sammy turned in early, and so did I. When I woke up he wasn't anywhere to be seen in our living area. So I checked back in the storage room. And there he was, about waist-deep in his latest project.

"Simeon!" he greeted me, looking a lot better than he had after meeting with Stone and Growly. "I'm glad you're up. Come here and hold this for me, will you?"

I wasn't half-awake yet, and still hadn't drunk a glass of water. But I didn't even think of protesting. Because what Sammy wanted me to hold in place for him was a piece of armor plate. And what he wanted to do while I held it was weld it to the absofuckinglutely coolest thing I'd ever seen in my life. It was a sort of mini-tank!

"I'll be right there." I declared, practically jumping through my own asshole I was so eager to get involved. What an awesome setup! Years ago, back when I'd been little, he'd bought a small earthmoving tractor-thingie from someone who'd lifted it Outside. I'd played on it for hours at a stretch, once upon a time; climbing all over the thing and tugging at the levers that made the blade go up and down. Sammy'd salvaged the heavy-duty battery-pack out of it for something or other, and I thought that was all he wanted. But now there were new batteries mounted on the back, the blade had become one of several pieces of armor-plating...

...and there was a geared spindle on top that looked to me as if it just might accept the autocannon!

"Holy shit!" I gushed as Sammy's welder snapped and spat. "I mean..."

"Heh!" the Wizard laughed. "I've named her 'The Arsenal of

Democracy'. Ain't she a thing of beauty?"

"Jesus!" I muttered as Sammy shut down his torch and lifted his face-mask. His armoring-job was clearly improvised. The tank's left side was shaped differently than the right because it was made of rusty old I-beams instead of concrete-filled pipe sections, for example. But good *god*, did the result look wicked!

"You get in and then raise the blade," Sammy explained. "That closes everything off."

I nodded, having already figured that out.

"The biggest problem is I can't get a full three-sixty traverse on the autocannon," he continued. "It'll only bear forward, luckily through a fairly large arc." He smiled. "The less people there are who know about that, the better. I'm gonna make it look like it'll spin freely."

"Right," I agreed. Then I shook my head and turned to face my friend. "There's no way you just pulled this design out of your ass. And half the parts are premade. You've been planning this shit for years. Haven't you?"

"Guilty," he answered, teeth flashing white through his long, gray beard. "Guilty as fuck, in fact. I've been looking forward to seeing it come together, too." Then he frowned. "Though, I'm having trouble with the secondaries.

"Secondaries?"

"Stenguns," he explained. "To cover the blind areas. So people can't just walk up and crawl all over the hull. I can't quite figure out the best places for them." He sighed. "When you're driving one of these things, Simeon, a Molotov cocktail can ruin your whole day."

I shook my head. Here I was on a lazy Sunday morning, still in my underwear, helping to build an honest-to-god tank. Judging by the Outside teen magazine Sammy made me read, most norm kids my age were either spending the morning watching holovid with their kid brothers or else taking tennis lessons. Life in the Zone might be a buncha shit in some ways, but at least it was *interesting*! "You," I said slowly, shaking my head, "are bugfuck nuts."

"Oh, yes," Sammy agreed, smiling and nodding - the happiest I'd seen him in years. Then he lifted the welding mask all the way off of his head. "Why else would I spend my life doing this shit? Come on, Simeon. It's past breakfast time and I haven't eaten yet either. Let's go take a break."

# Chapter Fourteen

Like so many other projects before it, the tank pretty much took over our lives. Sammy didn't sleep very well, so there wasn't any telling what hour of the day or night he might be found working out in the storage area, happy as a clam. He was considerate about it, working on quiet stuff like wiring while I was asleep, so I didn't have anything to bitch about. But there wasn't any doubt he was serious as fuck about what he was doing. Except for required reading, which I took care of during those few times when I was awake and Sammy wasn't, my schoolwork was suspended so I could help. I spent twelve, fourteen, even sixteen hours a day welding, testing circuits, and hacking some of the simpler software. To my surprise, Sammy didn't double-check much of my work unless I told him I'd had problems. "Shit, Simeon," he protested the first time I asked him to look over one of my circuits. "You're plenty good at that kind of thing. If you say it works, that's fine by me." That kind of scared me a little; the circuit in question was for a rear-view video backup feed. If it ever failed at just the wrong moment, people could be killed. So I'd gulped and double-checked it myself, half proud of lack of oversight but half frightened as well.

It worked just fine. Like most of my circuits did nowadays. Almost as many of them as when Sammy himself created them.

Towards the end of the project, things got kind of rough for Sammy. He had plenty of other shit to do besides build a tank. Like coming up with supplies from replacement grinding wheels to the daily fresh produce that kept me running. He'd always pushed himself as if he were one of his machines, but this time he went a little too far. One day when I woke up I couldn't find him anywhere. He was still in his grubby bedroom, it turned out, fully awake but weak as a kitten and covered in fine, cold sweat. "The pills," he whispered when I finally located him. "In the top drawer."

I didn't know shit about any pills, and suddenly finding myself scared as hell didn't do a goddamned thing for my deductive reasoning skills either. "What the fuck's wrong, Sammy?" I demanded.

"Pills!" Sammy roared. "Top drawer in the kitchen. Move your ass!"

That got me going. I didn't use the kitchen drawers often. Since I ate most things raw and whole, I didn't do much in the way of cooking. All I needed were plates, bowls, glasses, and sometimes a paring knife. But Sammy's chow needed to be heated and minced and chopped and ground and all kinds of other shit, so he had to keep a whole rollaway chest full of special cooking tools on-hand and easy to get at. Sure enough, when I checked there were pills in the top drawer; not one bottle of them but row after row. One bottle stood apart from the rest, its lid day-glow orange. I snagged it.

"Thanks, kid," he wheezed when I returned. Apparently I'd found the right one. Sammy poured three of the tiny red pills into his palm, swallowed them dry, then fell back onto his mattress.

"Sammy?" I asked. "Are you all right?"

"Sheeit!" he answered, already looking a little better. Whatever was in the red pills apparently worked fast. "Do I fuckin' *look* all right?"

I closed my eyes patiently. "Want me to get the doctor?" It was the middle of the night. But Doc Moses would come, I knew. Sammy kept all the shit in his office working for him. No other repairman would set foot inside the Zone.

The answer was a long, loud sigh. "Not this time," Sammy replied eventually. He sat up and shook his shaggy mane. "What time is it, anyway?"

"Three in the morning," I answered. "Are you sure about the doc?"

"I'm sure. He ain't gonna tell me nothin' I don't already know." Then he looked up at me. "Come on, Simeon. We've got some talking to do, shit I've obviously put off for too long already. Let's do it over breakfast. I'm not hungry, but there's always coffee. And teen-aged boys are always starved."

# Chapter Fifteen

I went out of my way to be extra-nice to Sammy as he groaned his way to his feet and made his slow way out to the kitchen. "I'll get your coffee going," I declared, racing ahead. Sammy never asked me to make his coffee for him, but I did it anyway sometimes. By the time I had all the fixings set up and the water heating, my mentor was seated at the table, looking much better but still far from a hundred percent. His eyes were filmed-over again, and the mere act of shuffling down the hall seemed to have exhausted him.

"All right," I finally said, plopping myself down across from him. My words were harsh, but their tone gentle. "What the fuck?"

Sammy smiled, but this time the expression didn't make him look any better. "I admit it, kiddo. I've been holding out on you. The old ticker's not in real good shape."

I nodded, but said nothing.

"Look it up on the 'net. It's called 'arteriosclerosis'. You don't see it anymore on the Outside, but living here has its little hidden costs."

I nodded again. "I already know what hardening of the arteries is."

Sammy smiled weakly. "Smart bunny!" He hadn't said that to me since I was little. "The doc can keep me going for a good little while to come. Maybe even for years. But I'm getting weaker."

I looked away. "What about Outside? What can they do for you out there?"

"It don't fuckin' *matter* what they can do Outside," he replied, eyes narrowing. For the first time, an ember of his usual internal fire flickered in them. "I'm Inside, and that's that."

"Right," I agreed, looking away. Sammy never went Outside. Or at least he didn't ever go Outside that I knew of. I'd asked him a few times why, but he wouldn't answer except to scratch my ears and tell me he loved me like a son.

Several long minutes passed before Sammy spoke again; he spent the time staring down at the tabletop. I took advantage of the opportunity to refill my friend's battered old Che Guevara mug. He nodded his thanks before speaking again. "I..." he said slowly, obviously seeking the right words. Sammy wasn't much for relationship shit. You had to judge him by his actions to appreciate what a stand-up guy he actually was. "I..." He was still too sick for this, I could see, so I tried to interrupt. But as soon as my mouth opened he silenced me with a slashing motion. "No, Simeon," he explained. "We've gotta do this. The sooner, the better."

I nodded again and held my silence. "There's all kinds of shit going on you don't know about," he said at last. The words seemed to be ripped from the very depths of his soul. "Shit I've mostly tried to protect you from. But I don't know how much longer I'm going to be able to."

"You don't have to..." I began, but then he gestured again.

"I've devoted my life... My entire life..." A tear trickled down his cheek. "And I've done *terrible* things. But all of them... You see, I wanted freedom for all of you." He wiped his cheek. "Your parents, Sammy... They were gold! Pure gold inside, just like you! You and your people, you have so much potential. And they made you *slaves*!"

"They made us to be slaves," I countered. "We wouldn't exist otherwise."

"To be owned," Sammy agreed. "It drove the cost of labor down to nothing, so once one country did it everyone had to. Some countries didn't want it to be that way, Simeon. But we had to follow along. In order to compete and stay alive."

I nodded; it was all in the history books.

"I was so proud of your parents," he continued, looking off into the distance. "They couldn't read or write nearly as well as you can. But their hearts were so true..." He shook his head again. "They'll be remembered, Simeon. I swear it. If it's the last thing I do. They were strong enough to free themselves. That's the key, we historians and anthropologists have learned. A people has to free itself. If others do it for them, they remain slaves inside forever Dependent on the society that freed them, in other words. Usually as a poverty-stricken underclass.

Then it can take dozens of generations to clean up the mess, usually through intermarriage and absorption. But your kind can never absorb. You're a different species." He lifted his eyes to meet mine. "Remember this always, Simeon. It's the most important thing I can teach you. Others can help you along the way. Provide skills and tools and coaching. But the final liberation has to come from within. It's as true for whole peoples as it is for individuals. Otherwise there can be no pride."

I pressed my lips together. This was growing awkward. "Sammy..."

He waved his finger one last time to silence me. "Things are coming to a head, son, and sooner than you might imagine. I want you to remember something for me."

"Sure," I agreed.

"Ralph Emory," he said. "Never forget that name. If you ever get into trouble and I can't help you anymore, go Outside and say that to a police snake. You hear me?"

I nodded. "Sure, Sammy. No problemo."

"Ralph Emory," he repeated, eyes blazing into mine. Then he eased back into his chair and sighed. "Don't be surprised at anything that happens after that."

# Chapter Sixteen

Whatever Sammy'd gone through, it sidelined him for a couple of days. I read and reread every heart-disease-related datapage I could find. The best thing I could come up with was something called a 'myocardial infarction', or 'heart attack', though it wasn't a perfect match for the symptoms. Possibly this was because all the pills Sammy was taking kept things from going as far south as they otherwise might've. There wasn't a lot to the article, mostly because a heart attack was listed as being a rare event in modern times. However, it urged the victim to seek immediate emergency medical help. And Sammy did let me go get Doc Moses for him the next morning, though he insisted that I lead him in and out through one of the secret entrances so that no one else would know he was sick. Sammy and the doc yelled at each other a lot, though I couldn't make out the individual words through the Doc's patient-privacy gadget. He stayed for almost two hours. When he left, he was seething. I'd never seen Doc Moses angry before; it wasn't a pretty sight. And, when I got back there were about a dozen new bottles of pills on the counter, half of them with orange lids.

Sammy might've been in a hurry to finish the tank, but flesh and blood has its limits. He was under strict orders to rest for a week. For the first couple days he did exactly that, moping around and thinking long, deep thoughts. At first he let me fix his coffee for him and such, but that didn't last. "Get out of here," he finally urged me after I burned his pancakes to a crisp for him one morning. I didn't get much practice cooking. "Go get some sunshine. Play your chinkgame, see your friends. You're not a decrepit old man like I am. It isn't natural you should spend all your time down here in a hole."

Rabbits love spending their lives in holes, actually. But I didn't correct him, because he was right. We were starting to get on each other's nerves and I did need to get out. Weiner and Peckerhead and the rest'd be worried sick about me. My legs also needed stretching. Deep down, I was feeling a terrible urge to dance. I checked the calendar; today was Friday. Perfect! There'd be plenty of dancers this evening, then. "You sure you're all right? And, you won't try anything stupid while I'm gone? Like, say, trying to weld on more armor plate all by yourself?"

"Heh!" Sammy smiled. It was almost as good as his old smile; the new pills were helping. "I'm just gonna sit here and surf the 'net, Simeon." He grinned even wider. "I'll be good! I promise!" Then, his features grew more serious. "Keep your ears open, too. We haven't heard back from our friends Stonecold or Growly. I find that a little... odd."

"Right," I agreed, smiling back.

"You go have a big old time," Sammy urged me. "I'll be fine."

## Chapter Seventeen

It was about ten in the morning when I finally emerged from the bowels of the earth and saw daylight again. "Heya, Gade!" The Rope greeted me with obvious pleasure, while mopping the floor. Apparently, The Warren's management was short on help this week so the doorman had to double up. He smiled and leaned his cleaning tool up against the wall, then extended a hand for me to slap. "Good to see ya, man! Where the hell've ya been?"

I couldn't help but smile back. "Big project," I answered. Then, I changed the subject. "So, what's the news?"

Rope's smile faded, and then he shook his head. "I dunno exactly," he answered, turning away. "But..." He sighed. "Something big's comin' down, Gade. You can feel it in the air, like."

"No shit?" I asked.

"Yeah," The Rope answered. "Every night there's all kinds of coming and going, most of it happenin' around Growly and his boys. The Avengers are in and out to see him two, three, six times a night. Even Zoomo dropped by once. A special truce was called, just to let it happen."

I gulped. That couldn't be good news! "No shit?"

"It's the word!" Rope answered. "Honest fuckin' injun." I looked away, and a long, awkward moment ensued. Then The Rope spoke again. "Somethin' else been botherin' me too."

My eyes narrowed. "Yeah?"

"Yeah." The black panther's brow wrinkled. "All of a sudden, Growly ain't got his own bodyguard no more. The Avengers are covering him." He shook his head. "I can't figure *that* one out for shit."

I blinked. Sure enough, when he'd come visiting Sammy with Stonecold, Growly hadn't brought a single soldier of his own along with him. Why hadn't I noticed that before? Did Sammy even know? The Rope might believe Adolph Hitler had killed George Washington, but he wasn't *stupid*. "Yeah," I agreed, nodding slowly. "I can't figure it either."

Rope sighed. "It's confusing as fuck. All I'm sure of is that when the shit comes down, I wanna be somewhere else." He met my eyes. "And you should be too, Gade." He shook his head. "Even the Wizard's gonna come out of this one ugly, I'll bet."

It was sunny outside, and warmer than it'd been in a long time. I hardly needed my coat, except to carry my gun and knife and shit. The weather was frickin' fantastic; on any other day I'd have been smiling and feeling all sappy, like. But not today, not now. My mind was too busy trying to fit puzzle-pieces together. What the hell was Growly doing walking around with an Avenger bodyguard? Why had the Avengers in turn granted Zoomo a truce to come a-visiting?

In other words: What the *fuck*?

Peckerhead and the rest usually spent all their spare time hanging at the chinkshop, scoring cheap prickgames and buying stick from Growly's dealers. And sure enough there they were sitting on the curb waiting for nothing when I turned the corner. Instantly they came to life. "Gade!" they greeted me, smiling hard and offering high fives. "It's the Gade!" "Renegade, where the fuck you been?"

I smiled back, even though the older I grew the harder it was for me to feel at home with these guys. Sure, they were canny enough, and quick on their feet - I couldn't use them for jobs if they weren't. They had perfectly good brains. But trying to talk anything but shit with them was hopeless. Sure, The Rope was full of crap in how he understood the world. But none of these guys, I'd bet serious money, even knew who the fuck George Washington *was*. I could shoot hoops with Peckerhead and Romeo and have a good time. But with every passing month shooting hoops and for that matter even playing chinkgames was growing less and less important to me.

I suddenly realized I was so lonely I ached. And yet...

"All *right*!" I greeted my friends with genuine enthusiasm. They might not be much, my little troupe. But their feelings, hopes and dreams were every bit as real as those of the fucking norm kids sitting in their college dorms listening to lame music and deciding which jacket to wear to dinner. And if they were dirty and larcenous and ignorant, well...they were *mine*, damnit! *My* people, *my* kind, rabbits like *me*. To be ashamed of them was to be ashamed of myself.

We slapped paws and high-fived and bumped into each other on purpose for a little bit, then Weiner finally spoke up. "Jesus, it's good to see you. We was gettin' ready to send out a search party!"

I smiled, but before I could speak Romeo cut me off. "Yeah, man. We need to talk to you, big time!"

"No shit." Peckerhead agreed. "We got problems, Gade."

I looked my friends in the eyes, one after another. Weiner was hurting for some stick, I could tell. He always was nowadays, and always would be until he died. The need was all I could see. But Peckerhead and Romeo, they weren't so far along. And in their eyes I read...

...fear.

"What?" I asked, remaining outwardly confident as I plopped down onto the curb, all thoughts of chinkgames now far from my mind.

"Everyone and their fuckin' brother's been asking us questions," Peckerhead explained. "Mostly 'bout you."

I nodded, but said nothing.

"Skulls," Romeo continued. "Avengers, independents, everyone." He shook his head. "They want us to tell every little fuckin' thing we know about you. Especially about what you can and can't do with tools and shit, and about the autocannon, too. They don't believe us when we tell em' we really don't know nothin'. Even though it's true!"

I nodded slowly. "I see."

"Everything's all fucked up," Weiner complained. "People used to respect that we were your posse and leave us alone, almost like we were hooked up with the Wizard too. Now the Skulls want me to join up. They want it real bad, Gade. The Avengers want me too. They say soon they'll make me an offer I can't refuse." His face screwed up. "And I can't score any stick!" he wailed. "Nobody'll sell to me, even though I still got plenty of money from the job."

"Won't nobody sell nothin' good to us," Peckerhead continued glumly. "Fuckers are trying to make a point. Break us, even," He nodded significantly towards Weiner, but said nothing.

"Shit," I observed, not really knowing what else to say.

"It ain't just us three," Romeo added. "Though we've got it worst. There ain't hardly no stick to be found, regardless. The price just keeps going up and up and up. It's fuckin' *bullshit*, man!"

"Somethin's goin' the fuck on," Peckerhead agreed, his voice lowered to a near-growl. "Somethin' big." Then he turned and looked me directly in the eye. "What the fuck is it, Gade?

"You ain't by chance holdin' somethin' out on us, are you?"

## Chapter Eighteen

I wasn't holding out on Peckerhead, though getting him to believe me took some doing. Scoring Weiner and the rest some stick wasn't particularly easy either, though I managed it. Henry Salvatore, the chinkshop owner, owed Sammy a favor or two for keeping his power on through some bad times. Since he also did a little small-time business in stick on the side, I figured he might be willing to ease Weiner's need. Assuming the request was framed properly, that was.

"You don't tell Growly!" the ancient norm sputtered as he pulled six syringes from behind his cash drawer. He *liked* having electricity, it seemed. I'd rather suspected he might feel that way. Even more, I'd been correct in my guess that he wished to continue having electricity in the future. "I'm not supposed to be selling to you no more. You furs are in deep shit!"

"Over what?" I demanded, handing one needle each to my friends and pocketing the other three for leverage later. They'd cost me almost all of my walking-around money, which by Zone standards was considerable. By then Weiner was shaking so hard that Peckerhead had to stick him, he couldn't do it for himself. Romeo, watching, looked at me and shook his head. Someday soon, Weiner wasn't going to be of much use to anyone anymore - including himself.

"I don't know." Henry declared, shrugging elaborately. "You boys always pay your bills and never steal. Not from me, anyhow. But the Avengers came with Growly!"

I nodded. Avengers and Growly, Growly and Avengers... Wherever I went, that was the new way of things. Stonecold's gang had always been the baddest in the Zone, or at least it'd been for as long as I could remember. That was because Sammy'd always propped them up. They took care of the school and shit for him in exchange for stenguns and other considerations. But now...

With Growly on their side too, maybe they thought they didn't need Sammy anymore?

Could it be that maybe they were sick of doing his odd jobs and following his annoying rules?

I didn't like to be around my friends when they were stuck. The dopey grins and manic, chemical-induced happiness made me feel a little sick inside. Peckerhead and the rest were so happy to have drugs again they didn't really give a shit when I left. They were behind me a hundred percent—I was their best fuckin' friend in the whole fuckin' universe. Which, an annoying little voice whispered in my left ear, just might have more to do with the three syringes still in my coat pocket than any less material source of loyalty.

I started playing with puzzle-pieces again as I walked down Ninth Street, not really paying much attention to where I was going. What the hell did the Avengers and Growly have in common, anyway? Stonecold's tribe were a buncha dumb fucks, really - dirty, diseased losers without much in the way of life expectancy. If they weren't such a bunch of bloodthirsty savages, they wouldn't count for shit in life—not even here in the Zone. But they *were* bloodthirsty—and how!—just like the Skullfuckers were bloodthirsty. There wasn't a thing to choose between them, in that regard. The gangs were about as primitive as a group of criminals could possibly get while still being successful enough to survive. Growly was of another sort entirely. Sure, he was as cold and cruel inside as Stone, and maybe even more cynical. The shit he put his hookers through, well... It was the stuff of legends. But he also had a brain, Growly did, illiterate or not. His strength wasn't measured in the number of stenguns or blades he could bring to a rumble. Rather, he was a businessman who employed no more muscle than absolutely necessary. He paid the Avengers well for stick marketing rights in their territory, and the last I'd heard he paid the Skulls equally generously. The whores were a sideline for him these days, more a personal hobby than anything else. His real income came from drugs; every time a fur in the Zone stuck himself a few coins made their way into Growly's pocket. Right at the moment there wasn't any stick on the streets. The lion, therefore, wasn't making any money. Yet he seemed happy as a clam.

It didn't make any sense at all. Unless...

Maybe Growly's sudden conversion to the Avenger way of thinking hadn't exactly been his idea?

## Chapter Nineteen

I didn't at all like where my speculations were leading me. Everywhere I looked the big power blocks that'd once provided the Zone with what little stability it'd known were slipping and sliding and turning each other on end. This was extremely dangerous, I knew. Even people like Growly understood that much. "Order," he'd explained to me recently, "is worth more than any one man's life." It'd always been so. The intellectual disorder of the Enlightenment spawned The Terror and Napoleon as well as George Washington, and the economic reordering created by the Industrial Revolution had energized the deadliest wars ever fought every bit as effectively as it'd defeated smallpox and leprosy. Something major was happening under the surface to bring all this shit to bear at once, but what? Sammy knew. He'd even dropped me half a dozen clues. He'd also, however, made it clear he wasn't gonna tell me. I'd have to figure it out for myself.

I scowled and kicked angrily at a little rock, it went flying off like a bullet. Here I was, damn near grown up and doing jobs on my own. In charge of my own little gang, even. And Sammy was still treating me like a little kid! What the fuck did he want from me, anyway? Why couldn't he just tell me the fuckin' truth instead of constantly playing mind games? And who the fuck was he, anyway, to ask me to write stupid papers and shit for him? Outwardly, I still appeared to be cool, calm and collected. In the Zone, that was the way not to be fucked with. But inside I was seething, frustrated, angry, jealous, tired of being number two...

"What gives, bro rabbit?" a voice demanded, seemingly out of nowhere. I started for an instant, caught completely unawares. *Holy shit!*

a little voice inside me screamed. *You're being mugged!* But in an instant
I was fine. It was only Shiv saying hello. I blinked and really looked
around me for the first time in many long minutes. Sure enough, I was
walking down Chestnut Street, in truce territory.

"How they hangin'?" Shiv greeted me again, smiling and showing
off his filed teeth. He knew full well he'd caught me unawares, so he
bumped into me to sort of rub it in. "You thinkin' them slow, deep book-
learnin' thoughts again?"

I smiled and shook my head. "Shiv..." I began. But, somehow, I
couldn't finish the sentence.

"Ha!" my one-time classmate replied, spinning in a circle as we
walked along for the sheer joy of it. "Ain't this some shit?" His smile
faded. "Right up until I scared the fuck out of you, I figgered you
might've come to see me."

I looked away. The last time Shiv and I had talked, it'd been about
pretty heavy stuff. Like, wasting our respective mentors and taking over
the Zone together. I started to speak, but Shiv cut me off. "All kinds of
shit be going down, Gade," he continued. "The Zone's getting'
dangerous, like." His eyes narrowed. "You ain't been talkin' out of
school, have you?"

Nothing, absolutely nothing, would more certainly shorten Shiv's
life than rumors getting back to Zoomo about a possible coup. "Nope," I
answered. Telling Sammy didn't count, I reckoned. He wouldn't sell Shiv
out, not over internal Skull shit. He believed fucking around with gang
politics was an excellent way to get one's self dead for no good reason.
"Let 'em waste each other from dawn to dusk," he'd told me once. "It's a
godawful shame, sure enough. But what the fuck can you do about it?"

"Good," Shiv answered, nodding slowly. Clearly, he trusted me. We
walked on a few steps in silence, and then he spoke again. "You do any
thinkin' 'bout my offer?"

I sighed. "I can't do it," I answered. "I mean..."

Shiv snorted. "You just ain't grown up yet inside, is all." He shook
his head. "Too much pussy-shit in your life, like books, teachers,
homework... You ain't had to get real yet."

I shrugged, but otherwise didn't answer. From his own point of
view, Shiv was probably dead-nuts right. We walked on a little further in
silence.

"Suppose someone else did the Wiz?" he asked. "What about then?"

I didn't know I had in me. In an instant Shiv was up against the wall, my blade at his throat. "That kind of talk," I explained slowly, "can get a man chilled. Even an old friend."

"Whoa!" Shiv answered, eyes wide in shock. "Hold on, Renegade. Just hold the fuck on!" He held up his hands so I could keep track of them. "Jesus fuckin' Christ! I didn't say *I* was gonna waste him. I ain't that stupid, bro!"

I scowled, then sheathed my knife and let Shiv loose.

"If I..." Apparently I'd caught my fellow rabbit completely by surprise-- he was still sputtering. "If I... You'd..." He shook his head. "If I wasted the Wiz, my life wouldn't be worth two shits. You'd hunt me down. Use that magic makes-you-sick crap on me. Or else shoot me in the dark." His eyes narrowed again. "And I can't just kill you both. I need you to make more stenguns. Like I said, bro, I ain't that fuckin' dumb." I nodded, legs still trembling from adrenaline overload. "But... Look, Gade. Don't get all excited on me again, all right?" I nodded again. "There's those who want to see Sammy dead. There always have been, you know. But all of a sudden, he's got enemies crawling out of the woodwork." He shook his head. "If he turns up dead, it won't be me that did him. I swear!"

"Who wants him dead?" I demanded.

"Everyfuckingone!" Shiv declared. "The whole fuckin' Zone's gone apeshit. Even the Avengers want his ass chilled. Though that's private information. Only we captains are supposed to know, nobody else." He looked sidelong at me. "And the stick's dried up, for everyone outside the Family. We've still got shit for ourselves. Not very damn much, though."

By that, he meant there wasn't any stick for anyone not sworn into his gang. "I've heard about that," I said.

"It's infuckingcredible," Shiv explained. "I can't figure it out at all." His eyes narrowed. "You read newspapers and shit. Is there maybe something going on Outside to dry up the flow?"

I sighed. "Not anything I've seen." I thought it over for a moment, then decided to prime the information pump a little. "Everywhere Growly goes these days, he's got an Avenger guard."

Shiv's face hardened. "That's it, then."

"That's what?" I demanded.

"What the fuck this is all about, man!" He shook his head. "Growly's the one with all the contacts, right? The only one who can bring stick in."

I nodded. "Everyone else who tries always ends up dead. Helluva coincidence, that."

"We Skulls still have stick," he explained. "But Zoomo, he's rationing it out, real tight. No one gets more than one needle at a time."

I nodded again.

"The Avengers, though..." He shook his head. "Look, don't tell anyone this, all right? Me and my squad caught one of the motherfuckers on our turf last night. He'd gone to see his squeeze, the dumb shit." Shiv shook his head in disgust. "He was just an ordinary soldier, no one special. We chilled him, hard. And you know what? He was carrying three sticks. Enough shit to last him a week, if he stretched it."

Suddenly, I was beginning to understand. "You Skulls, you're running out."

Shiv nodded, eyes hard. "Have you ever see someone try to function when they're in serious need? Much less rumble?" He shook his head again, then offered me his hand to smack. "I've gotta go talk to Zoomo, Gade. Right the fuck now. He's probably figgered all this shit out already, I know that." He smiled, exposing once again his crudely pointed teeth. "But I wanna see how just exactly how scared he looks when I tell him again. Ya never know when opportunity might come a knockin'."

# Chapter Twenty

It wasn't Saturday yet, but I was closer to the school than I was to home. Besides, I'd just spent most of a week underground building a tank out of scrap-iron and wet-nursing Sammy. So instead of going back home to do a little research, I decided to borrow Mrs. Rudder's study carrel.

It was her pride and joy that study carrel. The one segment of her little school with limited pretense to being up-to-date and modern. It worked off of the same stolen datafeed Sammy's machines did, and every few months he came by to install upgrades. Not that he was likely to be doing much of that again anytime soon, what with his heart going out and all. What would happen to the school once Sammy was gone, I wondered as I settled down into the too-small chair and began working while the littlest kids sang the alphabet song in the next room? Without his semi-magical protection, the very concept of maintaining a functioning school in the Zone was ludicrous. Mrs. Rudder's students paid if and when; the tuition-income probably wasn't even enough to support her, much less pay for desks and chairs and, most expensive of all, protection.

So where did the money come from, anyway? Somehow I'd never thought to wonder before...

The term "stick" was search-blocked on the mostly child-used machine; I had to reboot it with my own password before it'd let me look up the forbidden term. I'd never looked up "stick" before. Perhaps this was why. By the time I was old enough to be allowed, I already knew a lot more than I really wanted to about the shit.

There were about ten bazillion articles on the subject; I chose a general-interest piece. Stick, it turned out, was the most common street name for a highly addictive, tightly regulated drug frequently abused by gengineered sentients. The development of stick was generally seen as one of the worst abuses of the gengineered-slave era, as the drug had been deliberately and cold-bloodedly developed as a cheap and effective way to keep slave-labor populations docile and under control. Slaves would be addicted to stick as juveniles. Then the drug could either be offered as a cheap reward or else withdrawn as a punishment. The designed-in addiction proved to be so powerful, and withdrawal so unpleasant, that it was common for runaways to return voluntarily to the most horrific living conditions imaginable after a few days, merely in order to receive their injections. The Uprising had only become possible after alternate, illegal sources of stick were developed and became available to the slave population. Most commonly, illegal stick had been paid for by bartering stolen goods to the dealers, thus both furthering the spirit of rebellion and contributing to the anarchic, crime-ridden culture of the Treaty Zones to this very day.

Stick also had the side effect of notably shortening an addict's life. This had been considered a sort of free bonus by the drug's developers, who pointed out that this way aged and work-crippled slaves need not be either cared for, which was costly, or euthanized, which tended to intensify the political opposition to slavery. With the help of stick, slaves rarely lived much past their economic prime.

"Jesus fuckin' Christ," I muttered as I blanked the screen. The kids were all still in the other room with Mrs. Rudder, so there was no chance of them hearing me cuss. Though I wasn't sure why it mattered, since they heard and saw far worse every single day. Stick had been *designed*? The shit killing Weiner and more than half the furs I knew was, like, *on purpose*? Who the fuck could be *that* evil? I felt the fur rising along my spine in a rarely-experienced expression of rage. Fuckin' norms! No wonder we hated them so fuckin' much, the evil, miserable bastards!

"Are you all right, Simeon?" Mrs. Rudder asked, sounding worried. She'd snuck up behind me. "You look so... So..."

"Angry," I answered, turning around to face her. She was alone; the kids were singing by themselves now. So I was free to say what I thought. "Pissed as fucking hell, in fact. Does your kind have no fuckin' limits? Don't you have any decency at all?"

She blinked; it was the first time I'd ever cursed in her presence.

"Simeon, I..."

Then I realized how unfair it was to blame the world's shit on one of the few norms actively doing something to try and clean it up. "Fuck!" I muttered. "I mean.... Look. I just now read about stick, and what it was originally designed to do. I'm sorry."

Mrs. Rudder looked as if she'd just been hit. "You... I mean, you haven't tried..."

I closed my eyes, wanting to cry but somehow unable to. "No," I explained. "And never will. I just wanted to learn more about it."

She nodded. "Thank god." Then she looked away. "Stick might have been the worst of all our sins," she agreed. Tears were beginning to flow down her wrinkled cheeks. She'd been around the Zone every bit as long as Sammy I suddenly realized. And probably knew as many secrets. "My parents," I said slowly. "They were pincushions, then?"

Mrs. Rudder closed her eyes. "They were," she agreed. "All furs were. They *had* to be. It wasn't their fault." Another tear came leaking out. "We offered to help them out. Provide what they needed while they were organizing the Uprising. The addiction wasn't their fault, after all. But they quit instead. Both of them, cold turkey." She met my eyes again. "It was the bravest thing I ever saw. No one expected it of them. They broke free anyway, where few others have ever managed."

"Right..." My voice was calmer now. I climbed up out of the too-small chair, then looked down at my feet. "Mrs. Rudder..."

"Now, now!" my one-time teacher scolded me, forcing a smile. "There's no need to apologize, Simeon. You're growing up, is all. And facing ugly reality." Her smile faded, leaving her lined face looking ravaged and tragic. "Just don't curse in front of the children, is all I ask. Not because they don't know the words; I'm no fool, after all. But rather, Simeon..." She smiled again. "Because they look up to you so."

# Chapter Twenty-One

The Avengers hadn't treated me any differently than usual on my way into the school. Everyone present was a low-ranker and therefore probably not even aware of the bad odor Sammy and I were in with their masters. When I left, however, it was a different story. Stonecold was there personally, waiting for me along with his bodyguard. "Gade!" he greeted me from behind a false, Cheshire-cat sort of smile. Then he extended a hand for me to slap. This was a mark of great favor, one nearly everyone else in the ex-church would've given anything to receive.

I accepted the honor as politely as I knew how. "Stonecold," I replied. Then I put on my own fake smile. "What brings you to this part of town?"

"Business," he answered, gesturing towards a pew. The church was normally crowded to the point of bursting, but somehow an entire section had been cleared for just the two of us. "With you. We need to have a little private talk."

"He's carrying," one of the bodyguards objected.

Stone waved him off. "Renegade here is an old and trusted friend," he declared in a loud, penetrating voice. "A friend of every Avenger." He nodded to me. "Keep your gun. You're not going to try anything, here and now."

My mouth worked, but I said nothing as we sat down side-by-side on the worn-out old pews. "Gade," he finally said after a few long seconds of consideration. "I've known you since you were a little boy in diapers." He smiled. "I knew your parents, too. They were deeply respected."

Not respected enough to survive trying to regulate the stick trade, I didn't say aloud. "I respect you, too," he continued, "Immensely, in fact." He smiled again, wide enough this time to expose his long, pointed Bengal-tiger teeth. "I thought book-learning was just for pussies until I watched you grow up and pull off job after slick job. Especially this last one." He shook his head. "I'd make you an Avenger in a minute if you'd let me. You'd have your own squad from Day One. Your little posse'd be the core of it, if they'd join up too. Which I suspect they just might, considering. Them and more, all under your personal command."

I opened my mouth to speak, but Stone cut me off. "But you won't let me take care of you, Gade. And I understand that." He smiled again. "I mean, who the fuck wouldn't hook up with the Wizard instead, given a chance to learn all that magic shit? Plus he raised you, so it's natural you should have feelings for him." The smile faded. "Even if he *is* a norm."

It was my turn to sit in silence for a moment and think about what needed to be said. "He's a norm," I replied eventually. "But he's always treated me right. With respect even, like I was one of his own kind. He's never looked down on me because I'm a fur, I mean." I looked away. "They're not all motherfuckers."

"Maybe," Stone allowed, stroking his chin as if in thought. "And maybe not. Your parents were real close to Sammy, you know. Sammy and Alice Rudder both." He smiled again, looking very predatory.

"They engineered the local Uprising together," I answered. "Everyone knows. I think that's why Sammy never leaves the Zone. Maybe he's wanted Outside, for helping us." I shrugged.

"Oh, yes!" Stone agreed. "They organized the Uprising together, all right. They picked out your parents as leaders, and spent months grooming them for the job. Then they and the others like them picked a date and... Well. The rest is in the history books." He shook his head. "Or most of the rest is." He waited expectantly.

Despite myself, I felt my ears pricking up. "All right," I said. "I'll bite. What's not in the books?"

"Stick," Stone explained, spitting the word out as if it tasted bad. "Stick's not in the history books. Or so I hear from sources of my own." His eyes narrowed. "I was practically a boy, Gade. But I remember just exactly how it felt to wait in line every night after servicing my clients, screaming inside for a needle." He shuddered, then pulled out a stick and injected himself. "Now I can shoot up anytime I want. That's what it means to be free."

I shook my head and started to speak again, but once more Stone cut me off. "Oh, I know they fed you lots of happy horseshit about rights and elections and shit. I used to hear it all the time from your mom and dad, and I don't expect Sammy's changed much since then." His jade-colored eyes narrowed again. "But it's really all about stick. And, the Uprising only really changed two things."

"What two things?" I demanded.

"Firstly, we can stick ourselves as often as we can afford to nowadays. Whenever we want to, like I just said. If the norms want to control us they hafta try and do it with money now, which isn't nearly as effective. And second..." He grinned. "It used to be that we made our owners rich and didn't get shit for our efforts. Today we work just as hard as ever. But instead of our owners getting rich, it's the stick dealers." He smiled. "And you know who the very first to get rich were?"

I shook my head, even though I suspected what was coming. "Who?"

"Your beloved Sammy and Alice Rudder," he answered, slapping his thigh in glee. Then Stone pointed down towards the subterranean school. "How in the fuck do you think they pay for all their pretty toys, anyway? I've been in Sammy's lair too, you know, and I've asked questions in the right sorts of places. Those tools are top-fucking-notch! The money to pay for them comes right out of our pockets. We furs are still sweating to make norms rich, just like fucking always." His smile widened. "It's stick-money that's paid for all your highfalutin' books, son! Taken from dirt-poor pincushions, stumbling through the alleys and pissing themselves."

I pressed my lips together. "I know he sells guns," I explained. "And the ones who buy them get the money by selling stick. But..."

"But, shit!" Stone interrupted. "When Sammy and Alice first started out they were as broke as we are. Then all of a sudden you could trade stolen goods for a shot that didn't come from the masters. Everything the fuck changed then, practically overnight. And you know what? Something else changed overnight too. All of a sudden Sammy and Alice had money for their books and schools and to buy your parents free so they could work with them full time." He shook his head again. "It's so fucked up! We've just traded one owner for another, is all. And the new one's Sammy."

I sat in silence and thought it through for a moment. I'd just read that an alternate source of stick was essential to the Uprising. And, it did indeed have to come from somewhere. Which ipso-facto meant the income from its sale had to go somewhere, too...

It fit, damnit. And all too well!

Apparently it showed on my face. "See?" Stonecold crowed, slapping his thigh again. "They're norms just like all the rest. Fuckin' us every day of the week, rain or shine, and laughing all the while. They play teacher-games and shed crocodile tears about 'uplifting' us into a 'functioning' society, but their hands are just as dirty as mine." He shook his head. "As yours will be too, sooner or later. It's inevitable, Gade. Part of life in the Zone. Not your fault, not my fault. It's just what is."

Very slowly Stone stood up, then faced me. "Son," he said slowly. "The day's coming when you're going to have choose between the norms and us, and it's coming real, real soon." He bowed his head. "I meant what I said about respecting you and needing you on my side. You can keep the guns and shit flowing, should something bad happen to Sammy. And to be completely frank with you, something just might if he don't clean the shit out of his ears and listen to what I've been trying to tell him.

"But hear me, Gade. Be really, *really* careful about who you hang out with for the next little while. Whatever happens, there's going to be winners and there's going to be losers. Big-time losers. You absolutely don't want to be one of them. You dig?"

Involuntarily, my chin rose and fell in a nod." I dig."

"Good," Stone replied, looking a little less stern. "You're a smart kid. I don't have to explain any more." Then he smiled again, and patted me once on the shoulder. "Now, you're free to go. Have a nice day."

# Chapter Twenty-Two

It wasn't long before I had a pounding headache. Which I deserved, I supposed, for hunkering down so long in my little hole when I should've been up and about keeping in touch with shit. Now it'd all fallen on me at once and I felt a little overwhelmed. My mind was spinning as I sort of staggered down Chestnut, not paying half as much attention to what was going on around me as I should've. Instead all that penetrated were a series of everyday images; a young bunny-woman with a shabby stroller and two bags of groceries, walking close by an Avenger so as to take advantage of any protection his presence might offer, two young bunnies and a kitten playing at rumbling with trash-can lids and sticks, a Skull glaring at me suspiciously. Had the news that I'd just met with Stonecold traveled so quickly? Meanwhile torrents of information, illuminated by lightning-bolts of alternating terror and anger, stormed through my brain. My mentor was sick as hell, sure enough. He wouldn't last much longer even if he survived what was clearly about to turn into the mother of all rumbles. I had to think about what came next; even Sammy would understand that. The best way out, in theory at least, would be to find myself some kind of honest gig like The Rope had. It'd be boring as hell, and I'd live and die without ever making much of a mark on anything whatsoever, but at least it'd be safe. I wouldn't have to worry every single fucking day about taking a knife in the ribs, either. I could maybe find a nice doe and raise a little family...

...of foul-mouthed guttersnipes who couldn't read, got themselves hooked 'way too young on stick, would sure as shit end up in the Skulls or Avengers or whoever was running things twenty years from now, and probably brag all the while about how their sort-of granddaddy was the legendary Wizard who did magic and shit no one understood anymore.

And wasn't it sad that their father'd been too much of a pussy to follow in his footsteps? I shuddered at the image of my own children living the gangster life. It was just as well that the vision could never actually become reality. I was *far* too valuable a commodity to be allowed to go to waste mopping floors and shit for chump-change. If I even so much as made a convincing show of it, one of the gangs would sure as fuck convince themselves I needed to be chilled in order to prevent the other from obtaining my services. I'd watched Sammy tip-toe along the balance of power too long not to understand how such shit really worked. So in reality I effectively had my choice between the Avengers or the Skullfuckers. If I threw in with Stonecold, I'd never be my own man again. Sure, I'd receive the promised squad of subordinates. Stone would *insist* I accept them so they could spy on me and whisper back little snippets of information about how many stenguns I could *really* turn out if I wanted to, or about how I could maybe air-condition his digs too if properly persuaded. Bit by bit my squad of helpers would learn Sammy's magic from me until someone decided I didn't have enough left to teach to make putting up with me worthwhile anymore. Then said someone would chill me in the middle of the night, become Stone's new Wizard, and that'd be that.

On the surface at least, the Skulls were offering me a better deal. Zoomo was yesterday's news, even if he didn't know it yet. So his offer was just so much random noise. With someone like Shiv around, Zoomo's life-expectancy could be measured in months if not weeks or days. The Zoom was an old-school rumbler; hell on wheels with a noodge in his hands but not so good at thinking shit through. Shiv was the Skull's future, all right, and given time I'd figure him to take out Stonecold as well. In a lot of ways, Shiv was the finest thing the Zone could ever produce—the most any of us furs could ever hope to be. He was brilliant, daring, and ruthless; in another time or place he might've become a great conqueror of nations. Here and now, however, he had to settle for the Zone. With my help, the fact was he could probably take it.

I reckoned I'd do a lot better working with Shiv than with Stonecold; certainly I'd live longer. Because my one-time classmate needed me worse, I'd be able to set better terms. No squad, no assistants, no spies and interlopers. In his own twisted way, Shiv could even be termed honorable. He saw Zoomo as a fair kill because that was just the way the game worked; the Skullfucker's current top man had risen in exactly the same way, after all. So long as I never fucked with Shiv's power base and kept the stenguns and maybe a little trickle of other tech-stuff flowing, just like Sammy did, he'd leave me alone. I'd be his best buddy and right-hand man, in on all the major decisions. Shiv knew what gratitude was. Anyone not totally fucked in the head would grab the golden spoon and run like hell with it.

But I *was* fucked in the head. Or at least by Zone standards I was. It sickened me, the way the way Shiv filed his teeth into fake meat-eating points. He stank the deep ugly reek of the unwashed barbarian, and he killed as coldly and remorselessly as an epidemic. Yes, he was in many ways the best the Zone could ever do, our fucked-up society's ultimate product. Still...

The more I thought about spending my one and only lifetime forwarding Shiv's interests, the more I wanted to throw up.

It was still a gloriously beautiful day, sunny and unseasonably warm. One learned early in the Zone that life is a gift, not a right. In such an environment, it's wise to cherish every single day as if it were one's last. So I made a mighty effort to try and forget about Sammy's bad heart and about how much my future life was going to suck no matter what I did and about how just maybe the people I admired most in the whole fucking universe were as big a bunch of amoral assholes as Shiv. Instead, I held up my head, tried to appreciate the warm, fragrant air, looked up into the clear, blue sky...

...and saw a helo-bug coming around the corner, maybe forty feet up.

I gulped, then ducked around the corner of the nearest building. Helo-bugs weren't exactly everyday visitors to the Zone. The things were cop's eyes, and since there weren't any surface patrols anyway it was pretty pointless to waste such an expensive piece of equipment's time on us. After all, it could be better employed floating up and down in front of the rows of mansions and making the norms feel safer from us filthy criminal-types. I could think of only one recent crime worthy of the notice of a helo-bug...

Carefully, hand on my gun, I jogged down a narrow sidewalk that ran between two closely-spaced buildings in the direction most nearly opposite the bug.

"God damn norms!" the bunny with the battered stroller cried out behind me, shaking her fist at the helo. Then she saluted it with one finger.

"Fuck that thing!" an Avenger roared out,

"Amen, brother!" a Skullfucker agreed. Then he pulled out a stengun and fired a short burst. It missed, but the window-boards of the building across the street danced under the impact of stray slugs. The Avenger proved to be the better shot, however, or at least the luckier. His burst sliced the little robotic craft in two, then the two rival gang members danced a little jig in joy, high-fiving each other repeatedly. Fucking with the norms, apparently, was the one cooperative activity they were permitted to take pleasure in.

When I emerged from the little back-corridor, however, another copter was waiting for me.

The only thing to do was run. Helo-bugs weren't known to be armed, but the less they saw of me the better. So, I doubled back towards where a bunch of furs were clubbing the dead helo-bug in the middle of the intersection; with any luck, it wouldn't have been replaced yet. Sure enough, it hadn't been. I dashed across the street, abandoning all pretence of dignity and hopping like a rambunctious child towards The Warrens. Then, I rounded the corner...

...and almost skidded into, of all people, Fina.

"Simeon!" she greeted me, eyes widening in shock at my harried state. "What... I mean..."

There weren't any copters here yet, or at least none I could see. "Come on!" I urged her, taking her hand and tugging her towards the entrance to my home. "There's no time to explain!"

"What..." she began again, eyes still wide. Then, bless her, she quit asking questions and took off like a rocket, leaving me hard-pressed to keep up.

# Chapter Twenty-Three

I don't know just exactly why I asked Fina to run with me. I mean, I sort of liked her and all that. But if I'd taken time to think things through I'd have realized that getting her involved in my problems made even *less* sense when you took that into account. I was fucked in the head just then, was the real truth of the matter. Fucked and re-fucked, with a brain full of worries and terror and nowhere left to run in the larger scheme of things. So when I saw a friendly face, I just sort of glommed onto its owner and didn't look back.

I wasn't totally running blind, however. "Wait!" I cried, catching up with the surprisingly fleet Fina; it was amazing, how quickly she could propel all that plumpness. "This way!"

Sammy was far too cagey to live in a hole with only one exit; there were four entrances I knew of and I suspected a fifth which he kept secret from me on the entirely sound principle that what I didn't know I couldn't spill under torture. One of these entrances was located under a pile of garbage not far from The Warrens main door. It was only to be used in emergencies, because once its location became general knowledge it'd become worse than useless. In the distance, however, I could hear at least two more helo-bugs arriving. So far as I was concerned, that officially qualified my current situation as an emergency. "Here." I cried out, skidding to a stop. "Help me move this shit!"

"S-Simeon..." Fina objected, shaking her head. Obviously, she was thinking more clearly than I was. "I don't... I mean...."

Just then a little shadow flashed by as a helo took station near the entrance to The Warrens. "Shit," I growled again. "Come on! *Help* me!"

"I..." Fina objected. Then, reluctantly, she began throwing trash out into the pathway.

It didn't take long for us to expose the manhole; I hopped up and down on it twice, just like the stair-switch at our primary entrance. A little electronic brain recognized my body-weight and password. Then a loud click sounded.

"Simeon," Fina objected. "That's looks terribly heav—"

But before she could even finish voicing her objection, I'd thrown the counter-sprung lid aside. "In!" I roared, "Now! When you get to the bottom, don't move an inch until I tell you to."

Wordlessly and more than a little frightened, the doe complied. Once she was through I followed so closely I almost stepped on her head, throwing the "release" lever along the way. *Baroom!* the manhole-cover went as it slammed back home, creating echoes for what sounded like miles. It was now locked tightly into place once again. Even if I'd been seen, it'd take a man with a powerful torch many long minutes to cut his way through. Then there were the booby-traps.

For the moment, at least, we were safe.

"Simeon—" Fina protested again, but I held up a finger to silence her. A single red light glowed in the otherwise total darkness. I held my hand up to it and waited. Several long seconds passed while the security system reluctantly conceded that I was allowed access to this place, then the lights went on.

"Ooh..." Fina gasped, looking around in wonder. She'd probably expected to find herself in some kind of filthy drainpipe. While she'd gotten the 'filthy' part correct, this was no drainpipe. "It's an underground train station," I explained proudly. "The norms cut off service a long time ago and closed all the entrances. The tunnels and shit are all still down here, though. Hardly anyone even knows they exist. Everyone's forgotten."

"I sure didn't know," Fina replied, looking around with wonder. Being rabbits, both of us had a natural appreciation for well-executed tunnel-work. This was a warren on a grand scale indeed. "Underground trains! Wow!"

I smiled back, feeling a warm glow inside my chest for some inexplicable reason. "Don't tell anyone," I urged her. "This is one of Sammy's big edges. You can get anywhere from down here. If people find out..."

"Right," she agreed absently, still gazing around in awe. "Sammy's one of the good ones. I'd never do anything to hurt him." She looked at me. "Or you, Simeon. Especially, I'd never do anything to hurt you."

## Chapter Twenty-Four

I was still thinking about what it meant that Fina would never do anything to hurt me a few minutes later, as we sat side-by-side on Sammy's couch waiting for him. Where he was or what he was doing, I hadn't a clue.

"...so, yeah, I jacked the thing," I admitted to my seat-mate. "I'm guilty as hell, even, But... I lifted it from the norms, you see? Not anyone that matters."

Fina sat in cold silence as I babbled on, her legs crossed and her eyes looking off into the distance.

I sighed. "Look, Fina. I'm levelling with you here. I've stolen lots of stuff for Sammy. Cash, dead police snakes, computers... you'd be amazed. But never from anyone who couldn't afford to lose it. And never from anyone who treated us furs right."

Fina nodded slightly. "I see."

I sighed again, louder this time. "Mrs. Rudder knows," I explained. "Sammy doesn't just know-- he taught me how. Am I supposed to give a fuck about the norms when they don't care two shits about us?"

The doe's mouth formed into a thin, hard, hare-lipped line. "I suppose not," she said, finally meeting my eyes. "Everything's so messed up here. All the money's dirty one way or another. So, I guess stealing from the ones who messed everything up in the first place isn't so bad." She shook her head. "But, there is one thing bothering me, Simeon."

"What's that?" I asked, leaning back into the sofa's warm softness. Somehow, I felt a lot better inside, all of a sudden.

"You curse like a hard-core gangster," Fina explained, mouth hardening again. "I understand why you have to do that. It's because you need to look hard and tough in front of the other guys. Besides, Sammy cusses too when he works on stuff at the school, so I know where you picked it up from. But..."

"But...?" I asked, my ears suddenly drooping.

"But..." she continued. "I'd like you to stop, please. Around me, at least. It's terribly bad manners. And besides, you might slip up in front of the children someday."

I closed my eyes. Here I was with the Outside cops after me, two vicious gangs and three ganglords battling over my soul, and worried sick about Sammy. And this crazy doe was worried about my bad language! "Yeah," I agreed, looking away. "Sure."

"Simeon!" Fina complained, eyes flashing angrily. "You're not—"

Whatever it was that I wasn't, she didn't have time to say any more about it. Suddenly the phone rang. "Eep!" Fina cried, looking about in fear; clearly, she'd never heard such a sound before. It was almost true to say I hadn't either. Sammy was notoriously tight-lipped when he was away from his lair. A lot of the time he was sneaking around in places where extra noise or even a distraction could get him killed, or so he claimed. That was why he didn't want me calling him for anything short of a major fire. "Sammy!" I cried out, snatching the little cell-unit out of my pocket. My voice was quavering a little, I was so glad to hear from him. "Where the— Where are you?"

"Over at the Doc's, kiddo," he answered, cool and calm and collected like always. "He wanted to run another test, and we both had a little free time. Where are you?"

"Home," I answered. "With Fina." I paused a second to collect my scattered wits. "Geez, Sammy! Everything's going to sh—I mean, things are really bad, all of a sudden, all over the place."

"I saw the copters," my mentor replied grimly. "That's why I called."

"They were tracking me, I think," I answered. "Personally!"

"Yep," he replied slowly. "That wouldn't surprise me a bit. It's time to get you out, kid."

My brow narrowed. "Get me out? Sammy? What the—What do you mean?"

"I'll explain when I get there," he answered. "In the meantime... You said Fina is there with you? The helper-girl from the school?"

"Right," I agreed. "Her."

"Well," Sammy answered, his voice more cheerful, "We'll pull her out too then, if she's willing. You two just stay put and don't let anyone in. Like you need to be told that."

"Right," I agreed, feeling very lost. I hadn't needed to be told never to let anyone in since I was maybe eight.

"I'll be right there," Sammy continued. "You just—" Then there was a burst of stengun fire, followed by silence.

# Chapter Twenty-Five

"He said to stay put!" Fina wailed for about the thousandth time as I checked the magazine of the last secondary gun on our improvised little tank. The armor job wasn't quite complete; the back wheels didn't have shields over them yet and the top hatch had no dog to hold it shut. But, clearly, it was going to have to do. "I heard him as well as you did!"

"I suspect he may've changed his mind," I pointed out as I worked the stengun slide, a live round sliding into place under the firing pin. You had to be careful when you did that; stenguns were made to fall apart in nothing flat, which meant that perforce the workmanship wasn't of the highest quality. "You heard that noise at the end too, didn't you? Those were shots."

"Maybe it was one of the doctor's machines," she countered.

"Maybe," I allowed. "In which case I'm going to look pretty fu—I mean, very silly, driving down the street in this rig." Having gotten Fina involved in this mess was looking less and less brilliant every minute. I still didn't really know what to do with her, but for sure I couldn't leave her behind in the apartment. None of the entrances were keyed to her. If neither Sammy nor I came back she'd either die trying to get out or, eventually, of starvation.

"Is that the autocannon on top?" she asked, eyes wide. "The thing you stole, I mean?"

"Yep," I agreed, disconnecting the charging leads. Sammy'd gotten hold of a really nice set of batteries; I'd have enough power to fight for hours. "Isn't she a beauty?"

"In a deadly sort of way," she agreed. Then her eyes met mine again. "Don't do this," she urged. "Sammy wouldn't want you to."

"Probably not," I agreed. "But he's not here to stop me, now is he?"

I looked everything over one last time, then hopped up into the driver's seat. It was a long way to the exit, so I motioned for Fina to climb aboard as well. One man could fight the tank in a pinch, but two operators were better. The gunner's seat was very close beside my own. So close I could smell Fina's excitement.

"Wow!" she exclaimed as we began rolling down the endless tunnel. "I've never ridden in anything before. This is neat."

"Yeah," I agreed, feeling all warm inside again. "Don't touch anything, please. We don't want any accidents."

"Yes, Simeon," she agreed, sitting on her hands and practically purring.

The little tunnel we were following wasn't connected to the underground railway. Instead it slanted upwards for about a block, then ended in an armored roll-up door. The thing had originally been designed to protect the vulnerable supply-entrance to the fallout-shelter, and presumably was capable of withstanding a large blast. On the outside it'd been tagged so many times that the surface was almost indistinguishable from that of the equally graffiti-ed reinforced concrete all around it. Most people probably didn't even realize it was there. But Sammy kept it well oiled, and as part of the tank-building project he'd sent me to make sure the opening-mechanism still worked. I edged the tank up close to the wall, then reached out with a dowel-rod I'd brought along for the purpose and hit the "up" button. Slowly, without complaint, the door began to rise. A pincushion in the last stage of decrepitude had apparently been sleeping up against the thing; he stumbled to his feet and then staggered off, hands raised submissively.

"Wow!" Fina declared, eyes wide again. Then she turned back to me. "How are you going to close it behind you?"

I pressed my lips together. That was one of those little details Sammy and I hadn't quite gotten around to working out. "You see the other button?" I asked, pointing with the dowel. "The lower one?"

"Uh-huh!"

I self-tested the turret one last time; everything came up green. "I'm going to roll us into the street," I explained. "Then you get out, push the button, and run back outside before the door closes." I let my face harden. "If you get trapped in there, Fina, you could die. There's booby-traps and sh—stuff. Once you're out... Well, run for home and thanks for your help. Where I'm going, well,... It's no place for a doe." Then I smiled. "Besides, I like you. I like you a whole lot, in fact. And it'll be dangerous."

Fina looked away. "I'll get the door," she said. "But... I'm coming with you."

"No!" I countered. "You can't!" I shook my head. "Listen to me. If Sammy and I both get chilled, Mrs. Rudder will need your help more than ever."

Fina looked away. "If you get killed..." Then she shook her head violently and hopped down out of her seat. "Whatever, Simeon... Just, whatever."

"The bottom button," I reminded her, goosing the tank forward a little.

"I'm not stupid." she replied, sounding angrier than she really had a right to be. Or at least that I could see.

"I know," I said, rolling forward out into the daylight. "I just—"

Then something was hitting the side of my tank, like a handful of thrown gravel! Instantly I slewed the turret over to the left and looked through the camera-feed; it was a bunch of Avengers, all rabbits. One of them was hosing me down with a stengun.

"Hey!" I cried out over the loudspeaker. "Stop that! It's me, Gade!"

"Shit!" their leader replied. He was vaguely familiar, but I couldn't attach a name to the face. "It really *is* him in that motherfucker. Stop shooting, Boo!"

"*Eee!*" Fina squealed as she squeezed around the tank and sort of flowed up into the gunner's seat; with so much lead in the air I could hardly blame her. The inside of the tank was probably the safest-looking spot around. I rolled a little further forward so the door could finish closing, swinging to the left as I did to maintain the Avengers into my field of fire. At the same time I raised the big blade, sealing us in. Then I locked the cannon on the group's leader and selected "soft nose" and "wide dispersion".

"Where's Sammy!" I demanded over the loudspeaker. "What the fuck are you Avengers doing with him?" Fina looked at me reproachfully, then turned away.

"Now, Gade," the leader said, smiling and raising his hands. "Don't you be going all crazy on me, now." He stepped a little to one side; the cannon effortlessly tracked him. "This is just business, is all. Nothing personal."

"Don't you bullshit me!" I countered. "I know someone's tried to chill Sammy. And Stone was just threatening him to my face, not two hours ago."

"He also offered you one helluva deal," the squad leader added. "One I'd sure as fuck be glad to take if I was in your shoes." His head inclined slightly to one side. "I was just coming by to let you know the offer still stands. Stone said to tell you an unforeseen opportunity arose, and he had to take advantage of it. He's sorry he couldn't offer you more warning." The rabbit gangster eyed the tank again nervously. "Can you *please* point that big motherfucker somewhere else, maybe?"

"Maybe," I agreed. "Tell me Sammy's still alive, and I'll consider it."

The leader's face fell. "Gade," he said slowly. "I've always treated you right, man. We *all* have! But... I can't make you that promise. Not no more."

For a moment I simply sat there, totally at a loss as to what ought to come next. Then my decision was made for me. Someone was climbing up onto the tank from behind. In an instant, my hand flashed out and freed the secondaries. Their servos whined, and then they fired a short burst. "Mother fucker..." a voice screamed in agony. Suddenly, one of my cameras failed. All it would show was red.

"Gade!" the squad leader cried out, suddenly piss-your-pants terrified. "Don't! I mean, you don't have to..."

Whoever I'd just shot hadn't landed anyplace where I could see him; I solved that little problem by throwing the tank into reverse and backing up. Thump-thump went the suspension, cutting my victim off in mid-scream. The man I'd killed was wearing Avenger colors. Which was very bad news indeed for my friend the squad leader.

"Shit!" the man in the autocannon's sights cried out, the word seemingly ripped from the depths of his soul. "Shitshitshishit..."

All I had to do was flip a switch, and the autocannon, designed for easy remote-operation, did the rest. *Rrrripipip* it went, firing so rapidly no individual explosion was detectable. First the leader dissolved in a sort of red mist, then so did his companions. *Rrrripipipip*, and just that quickly and easily I'd wasted six furs, brother rabbits all.

# Chapter Twenty-Six

If one was going to rumble, I decided as I made my slow, bloody way towards the doctor's office, the best place to do it from was the driver's seat of a heavily-automated tank. I didn't have to kill nearly so many furs as I would've if the autocannon hadn't been such an impressive, showy weapon. I couldn't leave it on automatic all the time, because there were civilians all over the place. But whenever the Avengers formed a skirmish line and were stupid enough to try and stop me I chilled one or two or five or twenty and the rest fled in stark, raving terror. They were brave enough, the Avengers; they had to be or else they could never have gotten into the family in the first place. But fighting a faceless tank wasn't at all like looking someone in the eye while noodging their brains out or sinking a shiv into their guts. A few of the craziest, most whacked-out Avengers tried to swarm me at the corner of Tenth and Walnut, but the secondaries made short work of them. My biggest worry was that while I could at least be careful of where my strays were going with the main gun, the secondaries squirted lead all over the place without my being able to do anything about it. I thought of the stroller-lady and shivered; surely anyone who'd spent more than a few days in the Zone would be street-smart enough to take cover with such a big rumble going on? I certainly hoped so.

Walnut Street was chaos even before I arrived. Avenger corpses hung from every telephone pole. These included, I was saddened to see, that of Doolie the greyhound, who'd been such a good, fair-minded watchman. Like most of the others, a nail was driven into his head. The street was chock-full of black-and-white clad Skullfuckers, swirling about everywhere and looting Joe's Superama. From time to time bursts of stengun fire broke out for no apparent reason.

"Sammy." I heard a familiar voice shout through the din. "Sammy? Gade? Are you in that motherfucker?"

I fumbled for the bullhorn switch, a task made all the more difficult because Fina had grabbed my right arm with all of her strength and wouldn't let go. She was absolutely terrified. But what could I do? Put her out into *that* madness? "That you, Shiv?" I asked, searching for and finally finding him with my main camera. "This is Gade. I think maybe Stone tried to put a hit on Sammy."

"Makes sense," Shiv agreed, easing up next to my vehicle's left side. He was carrying not one but two stenguns, and was spattered in blood. "They pulled a bunch of soldiers out of the treaty zone, so with a big fight coming on anyway we swarmed them and whipped their asses." He raised his arms and made vulgar Skullfucker finger-signs with both hands. "Yee-hah!" he roared. "Fuckin' wasted them all! I didn't think old Zoomo-pussy had the 'nads. But when his chance came..."

I nodded silently, putting two and two together. Most of the Avengers were probably over at Doc Moses's place, making sure Sammy was thoroughly chilled and planning a counterattack. "Where's Zoomo?" I demanded. "I need to cut a deal with him. Right fuckin' now!"

"He's hurt," Shiv replied. "Hurt bad, Gade." He smiled his false-fanged smile, looking not the least bit bereaved. "I doubt he'll make it through the night. He took a ricochet in the head and now you can see his brains. We can't even get him through Avenger lines to see the doc. Terrible shame, huh? Not that it'd do him much good anyway."

"Are you the man, then?" I demanded. "If not, who is? I'm tellin' you, I've gotta make a deal right now!"

Shiv scowled in concentration. "I reckon I am," he declared eventually. "If not, I will be by dark. There's a couple other ambitious types who need to be dealt with, but nothin' I can't handle. In the meantime the soldiers will go where I tell them to go and do what I tell them to do when they get there."

That was good enough for me. "Sammy might still be alive," I explained. "I want to get him out, if at all possible. He's at the doc's."

"Sheeit!" Shiv declared, rolling his eyes. "Do you know how many motherfucking soldiers the Avengers set on him?" He shook his head. "I want a deal, Gade. Really, I do. But Sammy's a dead man."

"Maybe," I agreed. My mentor never traveled without a few

surprises in his coat and the doctor's office was fortified in ways no gang-banger could possibly foresee. "Or maybe not. If he's already gone, Shiv, I won't blame you. We'll work something out in that case. But for now..." I waggled the turret a little for emphasis. "There's Avengers we both agree need wasting, and we're just standing here fucking around."

Shiv's grin widened, and his eyes sort of glowed. "Fuckin' A!" he agreed. "Friend, you have just struck yourself a bargain. The details can wait." He slapped the side of my vehicle. "Besides, I want to see this ugly son of a bitch in action!"

# Chapter Twenty-Seven

Shiv's wish certainly came true. He'd hardly rallied his forces before the inevitable Avenger counterattack came roaring in. The assault was delivered with determination and in force, and I don't want to think about what might've happened had the Skulls' new leader not already gotten his troops back into hand. If the Avengers had caught the Skulls still rioting and milling around like idiots celebrating their earlier victory, the sudden blow would've swept the street bare.

My tank helped a lot too. Fina still wouldn't let go of my right arm, and since the vehicle really needed a crew of two anyway, I had a pretty hard time keeping up with the rapidly-changing situation. Once I even accidentally ran down a Skull who was trying to protect me from one of the many attempted close-assaults. He screamed, and then Fina joined in perfect harmony as I rolled remorselessly on. But what else could I do? I hadn't killed the Skull on purpose; it'd been an accident, pure and simple, caused by the fact that I could only do so many things at once.

By the time we turned onto Eleventh, where the doctor's office was located, I was growing very worried indeed. Sammy'd manufactured thousands of new soft-nose rounds for the autocannon; our lathe had been doing little else for days. But now I was going through the things like shit through a goose. Only twenty percent of my initial soft-nose load-out remained by the time Doc's office came into sight. I still had the specialty-stuff on-board, true enough. But soft-nose was my bread-and-butter. If it ran dry, I'd suddenly find myself armed solely with a slow-moving ram. Would twenty percent be enough? I could only hope.

We caught the Avengers besieging the building by surprise; they either weren't expecting us so soon or perhaps not at all after their savage counterattack. All of them had their backs to us, gaping open-mouthed at the clouds of ugly yellow-green gas pouring like smoke from the lab's windows. I grinned and swung wide around the corner, my near-silent electric motors not making enough noise to distract them from the colorful spectacle. It was chlorine gas; there were huge bottles of the stuff hidden all around our workshop. Obviously Sammy'd used it to secure Doc Moses's place of business as well. He'd taught me all about chlorine and explained that while there were more potent war-gasses, in this application the color was an essential part of the terror effect. "In a real war, a little green shit in the air wouldn't scare anyone," Sammy'd explained. "But here in the Zone where they don't understand nothin'..." Then he'd grinned like a savage, and I'd smiled back with equal delight.

I wasn't smiling now, however, as I sat and watched a group of Avengers burst out of the building's main door and collapse onto the sidewalk, writhing and convulsing in agony. Meanwhile, more heavier-than-air chlorine fell out of the shattered windows and continued to smother them. It was ugly, brutal, obscene... Even worse than the spike-brained corpses the Skulls left dangling in their wake. This was self-defense, I understood. Sammy hadn't started this fight. He'd been avoiding it for years, even. And the man was up against desperate odds. Still... It was the blackest of black magic. Something I hoped I'd never, ever have to look upon again.

Just then a fierce roar erupted from behind me. While I'd been surveying the office building, Shiv had taken more positive action. He'd massed his men into a single angry stengun- and noodge-brandishing body, and was leading them in an insane, courage-building chant. "Fuck their skulls! Fuck their skulls! Fuck their skulls!" My former classmate still didn't have nearly so many soldiers at hand as Stone did. On the other hand Stone didn't have a tank on his side. So I reckoned the odds were fairly even. Then I frowned, and decided it was time to begin my own part in the festivities.

Off to the building's left, near what was once a bus shelter but was now an improvised home for perhaps a dozen down-and-out pincushions, stood a group of Avengers waving their arms and shouting at each other. Leaders, I decided, trying to deal with the fact that Sammy had proven so unexpectedly difficult to kill. I offered them soft-nose, wide dispersion to help them settle their argument. Two managed to duck quickly enough to find cover behind the thin metal of the bus shelter. I switched over to armor-piercing, and that was that. Meanwhile, Shiv took my fire as a signal. "*Fuck 'em!*" he roared, bouncing up and down like a child. With an ugly roar his black-and- white-clad soldiers surged forward, forming a sort of wedge with an enormous noodge-brandishing anthro-buffalo at the apex. "Fuck their skulls!" they continued to chant as they advanced in a sort of filthy, depraved stampede. "Fuck their skulls!"

Because Shiv's gang stayed clustered together, I was able to keep firing right up until the two sides slammed into each other with an audible impact. Stenguns ripped, improvised spears stabbed, bloody noodges rose and fell. All the while I did my best to seek out clear targets wherever I could-- mostly little groups of Avenger latecomers and lookouts arriving to join the desperate party. The soft nose ran out pretty quick, so then I used up the non-penetrating fragmenting-bullet stuff picking off window-perched Avengers armed with stenguns. They were pouring magazine after magazine into the main battle down below, probably wasting as many Avengers as they were Skulls. Still, it seemed prudent to shut them down. Then, when a group I thought was part of Stonecold's bodyguard came running down an alley, I hosed them down with the tear gas rounds. Tear gas projectiles were intended to be fired in front of a group one wished to stop. But, because I was trying to do too many things at once, I slipped up and targeted the burst directly on their bodies. The low-velocity, non-lethal rounds barely penetrated the skin, then burst and spewed forth their burning, caustic contents. The results were, well...

No one else tried to come down *that* alley. Not after that.

Then I was out of ammo entirely, and helpless. For a minute or two I simply sat, stunned, as the battle swirled and raged around me. Then another chlorine-gas charge burst up in the doc's office, and I knew what I had to do. "Hang on!" I ordered Fina, my voice low and gruff. "I'm gonna go get Sammy."

# Chapter Twenty-Eight

The Skulls had attacked in a single coherent mass, but now the fighting had broken down into what amounted to an epic free-for-all. Little knots of Skulls and Avengers cursed and whirled and fired at each other in reckless abandon. The pavement was littered with corpses and wounded. Meanwhile, up above, at least a dozen helo-bugs danced a complicated waltz, each striving to offer its norm master a ringside seat. My guess was the footage would sell for millions. I tried not to run over too many bodies, either living or dead, as I edged my way towards the brawl's epicenter, the space right in front of Doc's front door. But I did have to crush some, so I just did my best to make sure they were Avengers. Bullets were pinging off my armor like a hailstorm, but I tried to ignore them. "I've got to go in there," I explained to Fina. "I've just *got* to. No one else knows about chlorine gas."

"No!" she screamed, as the secondaries spoke again. Apparently, someone who hadn't gotten the word yet had tried to climb aboard. "You're not leaving me here. You *can't!*"

I pressed my lips together. There was, I had to admit, considerable justice in her position. With every passing minute, my idiot decision to involve Fina in this mess was looking dumber and dumber. If we got out of this, I swore, I'd never look at a doe again. They made me stupid. "All right," I said finally. "When we move, we move fast. There won't be time for questions."

"Okay," she agreed.

"That green stuff," I continued, "is a gas. Not magic, see? Just chemistry, and water neutralizes it." I took my shirt off and ripped it in half, then reached under the seat for the gallon jug I knew was there.

"We'll be fine, so long as we keep these over our faces." Except for the bullets and shivs and such, I didn't add.

"Uh-huh," she agreed, rather shocking me by snatching the cloth out of my hands and soaking it down for me. "Have you got a spare knife?"

I blinked then handed over my switchblade. "You know how to use one?"

"Oh, *please*!" she answered, rolling her eyes. "I have three brothers."

My eyebrows rose, but I didn't comment. There wasn't time. "This used to be an earth-mover. I'm going to use the blade to bash a hole in the wall, and then before anyone figures out what's going on we'll duck inside. Once we're in, we're going to go upstairs and find Sammy. The doc too, if we can. Then we're gonna drag them out, load 'em into the tank, and head back home to wait out the storm. Anyone gets in our way, we waste them."

"Right," she agreed, expertly folding my ruined shirt into two improvised gas masks. Apparently she felt better with something constructive to do. Maybe I should've tried to teach her the basics of serving as a gunner after all? "In, make the grab, and out."

"Good," I agreed, twisting the tank's speed control as far as it would go. "Let's do it!"

We hit the building much too hard; I'd meant to merely open a small hole, but miscalculated. Between the mass of the earth-mover itself, the added tons of welded-on armor and the smaller but still non-negligible weight of the autocannon itself, the impact when we hit the blank area of wall I'd chosen nearly proved fatal to the entire structure. Bricks came pouring down on us like rain, knocking out all of my cameras, and the secondaries chattered away in a mad effort to ward off what they interpreted as a massive close assault until they either jammed up or ran out of ammo. I thought for a moment that we were buried alive. But the blade moved when I threw its lever, though very reluctantly. And, when it did, green-tinged daylight appeared beyond.

In an instant we had our wet rags on and were walking through a charnel house. Doc Moses's office was located on the second floor, and I already knew there'd been close-quarters fighting because of the way Sammy's phone call had been interrupted by gunshots. But I'd never imagined...

It was *awful*. Whoever'd planned the hit couldn't have known about the gas-defenses. More likely, he hadn't even known what gas was. He *had* been aware, however, that the Wizard was the toughest, canniest, hardest-to-kill being in the entire Zone. So, as near as I could guess, he'd compensated for the danger by packing the house with as many Avengers as he could before striking. It'd probably seemed like a good idea at the time, but the result was appalling. You could see where the gang-mates had fought, clawed, stabbed and shot each other, trying to get away from the sudden choking green cloud descending from what must've seemed like nowhere. The dead were plied three and four deep by the windows and doors, so that their bodies had kept anyone behind them from getting out. The rest, who died from the chlorine...

...well, that was even worse.

Fina flopped enough bodies out of the way for us to get to the stairway, while I stood and covered her with my little pocket-pistol. Being intended as a last-ditch weapon, it held only four rounds. Like an idiot, I'd left my rifle back in the shop.

As near as I could tell everything on the first floor was dead, all the way down to the flies. But chlorine sinks; things might be very different up above. "Sammy!" I cried out, pointing my weapon up the stairs and advancing cautiously behind it. "Are you up there?"

No one answered. Which was sensible enough, I supposed, since the biggest rumble there'd ever been was still creating a deafening roar just outside the shattered panes. Most likely, no one could hear me.

So, I edged up a few more steps, almost to the top with Fina just behind me. "Sammy?" I was all the way past the stairs and around the corner, contemplating the locked steel door of Doc Moses's office, before anyone replied. And then, the voice came from directly behind me.

"It's no use, kid," Stonecold gurgled. Clearly, he'd inhaled some gas, "Drop the gun. We've got you covered."

# Chapter Twenty-Nine

I complied, not needing to be told twice. The little gun, a constant companion since my thirteenth birthday, clattered uselessly to the ground.

"That's good," Stone said. The floor creaked, and with a muffled groan of pain the big Bengal tiger climbed to his feet. "*Real* good! But you're a stupid fuck after all. Turn around."

I did, and my heart sank. There wasn't anyone else, just Stone with a stengun. The rest of his bodyguard was lying dead in an untidy pile behind him. Even the ganglord himself was bleeding from a dozen wounds-- it looked to me like he'd been formally introduced to the twelve-gauge zip gun Sammy carried under his coat.

...which meant Sammy was alive, I suddenly realized. Or, at least he'd survived the initial assault long enough to shoot back.

Stone grinned, exposing a newly-broken fang. "This was a dangerous hit," he explained. "Dangerous as fuck, in fact. If I hadn't led it in person, people would've gotten ideas." Then he raised his voice. "Oh, Sammy boy! You'll never guess who just wandered in. Wanna make a deal for your boy-wonder?"

My heart leapt with joy; maybe he was still alive after all! But Sammy didn't answer. "Gah!" Stone complained, turning towards me. "I can't afford to leave him alive behind me. But on the other hand..." He shook his head, and then coughed violently before shouting even louder. "Hey, Wizard!"

Again, there was no answer.

What came next took me by surprise, though it really shouldn't have. My left shoulder exploded, then I found myself rolling around on the floor, screaming. God, how being shot hurt! "Sammy!" Stone called out again. "You want to come the fuck out *now*, you son of a bitch?" Then came another explosion, and a ball of agony detonated in my left calf. "I got all day, asshole." He stepped forward as if to pound on the door...

...and a long burst of stengun fire erupted from downstairs, striking home inches from Stone's elbow.

"I'll fuck your skull, asswipe!" Shiv screamed. Apparently the gas was thinning out down there. "Gade, you all right?"

I tried to speak. But *"Aaah!"* was all I could manage.

"Shiv!" Stone greeted his enemy. He pointed the stengun back at me. "Let me guess. You need this little fuck alive too. And on *your* side. Or else your whole world's gonna fall apart."

"Don't kill him, man!" Shiv demanded, stepping out to where both Stone and I could see him. "Don't fuckin' do it! Or else I promise you'll die slow, you prick. We're winnin' out in the street. And I *keep* my fuckin' bargains."

"Maybe you're winning," Stone answered. "Or maybe not. I can't rightly tell. But I do know one thing for fact, which is that I'm *sure* as fuck the boss in here!" The Avenger's leader swung the stengun towards me, his face screwed up as if he were about to have another coughing fit...

...and in a blur of motion, Fina danced in, hopped up high, and sank my blade up to the hilt into Stonecold's neck.

*"Fuck!"* his lips said, though no sound emerged. Then his eyes darted back and forth between me, and Shiv and Fina, clearly unable to decide who to shoot first. Finally he settled on Shiv, who was now rocketing up the stairs and screaming an enraged, inarticulate battle-cry. The dying tiger squeezed the trigger...

...and Shiv fell backwards down the stairs, flopping end over end like so much breeze-blown laundry.

I tried to get up, but my arm and leg wouldn't work and it was getting harder and harder every second to think. Now Stone was turning on Fina, and his gun was rising again. "No," I tried to object, raising my good arm and feebly grabbing at Stone's ankle. But somehow, no sound would come out. "No!"

The gun continued to rise, Fina's face formed a mask of defiance and rage...

...and the door to Doc Moses's office flew open. There a bloody, battered, parchment-skinned Sammy stood, hefting a stengun of his own. Unlike Stonecold's, Sammy's weapon was already raised. He emptied the whole clip into the tiger, practically cutting him in half.

"Sammy..." I croaked, smiling and extending my good hand towards him. "Thank god!"

He looked down at me, smiled, tried to reply...

...then fell flat on his face and moved no more.

# Chapter Thirty

The fighting outside roared on and on. Meanwhile Fina wailed and cried and tried to bandage me up as best she could. "It's all right," I kept trying to tell her. "Everything's going to be all right." Apparently, either I was slurring my words so badly she couldn't understand me, or else she figured I was just trying to reassure her. Imagine that! At any rate, the slug in my shoulder had penetrated deep, probably much deeper than Stone had intended. There was a spray of blood whenever I exhaled now, and just past Sammy I could see Doc Moses lying dead on his clinic floor. Without his help, I didn't have a chance. Worst of all, Fina knew it too. Finally, she gave up trying to plug the leaks and sat cradling my head in her lap.

"G-g-get out of here," I stuttered. "I'm s-s-sorry..."

But my words didn't have the desired effect. Instead of abandoning me, she hugged me again and wailed louder than ever. "I was a fool!" she shrieked. "A fool to dream,! There is no God—there *can't* be, if our misery means so little! What kind of god doesn't even allow His children to hope?"

I sighed and looked away. I'd hurt Fina, hurt her badly. Of all the things I'd ever done, that was the one I regretted most. "I..." I began again. "I..."

Then something caught my eye. A helo-bug was floating just outside the broken office window. This one was painted olive-green, not police blue like all the rest I'd ever seen. Sammy'd given me a password, once - a name to say. And helo-bugs, like police-snakes, could hear an ant fart. "Ra...." I stuttered. "Ra..."

"Oh!" Fina wailed, covering my mouth. "Save your strength,

hon." I shook my head angrily. "Ra..." I tried again. But the words just wouldn't come. It was too little too late - the story of my entire life. Then in the distance I heard an angry thumping sound rapidly growing until it filled the entire sky. "Norms!" an angry voice cried, out on the street. "The norms are coming!"

"Fuck!" an angry voice replied. "Hundreds of them..."

"They're darkening the sky." a third added.

The sky was darkening, all right; it was fading to black, just like everything else. If the norms were coming, that was someone else's problem now. Not mine. I had no problems left at all, except for one. I'd done Fina wrong, very wrong, and knew only one way to make it up to her.

"I love you," I said with silent lips, just as the lights finally went the rest of the way out and heavy automatic weapons began spraying down the pavement outside.

## **Chapter Thirty-One**

I woke up lying in a white-sheeted bed, in the funniest-smelling room I'd ever been in. It would've scared the shit out of me, except it happened slowly over a period of hours if not days. I'd sort of halfway come around, not really knowing if I was dreaming or not, then go right back under. A couple of times when I came to I thought Fina was standing there. Then I'd scream and holler, because if she was there it meant she'd been killed too. Which was no one's fault but mine.

Eventually, however, I finally woke up for real. By that time I'd done enough of the half-awake nightmare stuff to understand that this was a hospital and the tubes coming out of me were for drugs and shit. I blinked a couple of times, looked around me...

...and a norm every bit as old as Sammy was sitting next to me in a chair. "Hello, Simeon," he greeted me. "How do you feel?"

"Like shit," I muttered, trying to raise my head a little. This made my shoulder seem to catch on fire. So I just laid back, helpless. "What do you care?"

"More than you might think," he answered. Then he smiled. "If you need a nurse, I'll call one. They told me that because you're so young and healthy the repair-bots are working fast and except for some pain, you'd probably be clear headed when you came around."

I tried to shrug, failed, and then expressed my contempt by looking away.

The norm sighed. "This is awkward, Simeon, very awkward indeed. First, let me tell you how sincerely pleased I am you're still with us." He shook his head. "You probably don't believe me, but when I saw the remote-image of you lying there in a pool of blood alongside Doctor

Kiel, well..."

"Doc Moses, you mean," I corrected him.

"No, I meant Doctor Samuel Kiel, one of the greatest revolutionary anthropologists who ever lived, in my somewhat-biased opinion." He smiled. "By the way, your paper on the Industrial Revolution was remarkable for someone your age, particularly the bit comparing the disturbances of 1848 to your own June Revolution. I've received far worse from grad students. Though, Sammy was right. You really aren't supposed to use the word 'fuck' in a formal paper."

I blinked. "What is this shit?" I demanded, trying to sit up again, but failing. "And who the hell—"

"Now, now," the norm objected. "Please, don't get all excited. It's bad for the 'bots."

I laid my head back down, but maintained an angry glare. "What the fuck?" I demanded again.

The norm sighed. "In your life," he said eventually, "quite obviously, all has not been as it appeared."

"No shit, Sherlock," I answered, scowling just as hard as I could. "Are you the one who got my parents wasted, then?"

The norm winced and looked away. "No," he said eventually. "That was.... Unforeseen. A failure, a calculated risk that went bad." Then he met my eyes again. "One they both knew of going in, upon my word of honor."

I looked away, but said nothing.

"Sammy was proud of your paper, Simeon. That's why he sent it on to me. Proud parents often show off their kid's papers, you see. And proud college professors show off these same papers to other professors. I've seen rather a lot of your work." He smiled again. "Sammy and I have a lot in common, you see. We're colleagues in more than just a professional way." His smile faded. "I presume he taught you about the Underground Railroad?"

I knew he didn't mean the tunnels under the shop. "Yeah," I agreed eventually.

"They did a lot of good work, before the Civil War. Freed a lot of slaves." He smiled. "And helped set things up for the Emancipation Proclamation."

I nodded, carefully due to the pain.

"He and I and a few others, including your Mrs. Rudder, formed a similar group oh... about thirty years ago now, with the same name. We didn't think slavery was a good thing, no matter if the slaves were animals or human or a mix." He looked away. "We also suspected your kind was far more capable intellectually than you'd been given credit for. That's another reason Sammy was so proud of your paper."

I nodded again, but still said nothing.

"Anyway... We took it upon ourselves not to free you, which never works out, but rather to help you free yourselves."

"Right," I agreed. "And that's why you drowned us in stick. To make us free... Made it so you'd get rich off of the shit. While we died young, broke and ignorant."

The norm's face colored. "We had to develop alternate sources," he admitted. "And, we were operating underground. Illegally, though there was a lot of public sympathy behind us. So we had to work with what contacts we could make." He sighed. "Things got out of control. A lot of good people died, and are still dying. Outside as well as Inside, I might add." He sighed. "It's a good thing you ran from those first copters, Simeon. They were operated by the local police. They'd have killed you if they'd caught you."

I blinked. "For stealing an autocannon?"

"No. For working with us and thereby in the long run threatening the existence of the illicit stick trade. Now that the Uprising is over, we've gone legitimate. Because enough people think we did the right thing back when it was illegal to stand up for the furs, we now hold a majority in the government." He grinned. "It shouldn't surprise you that trying to clean up the mess we made of things in the Zones is number one on our agenda."

"I... Uh..." I shook my head to clear it, and to hell with the pain. "I mean, why don't you send in the troops, then? Impose order at gunpoint, and all that shit?"

"Because it's only a short-term solution. We could keep order for a few months at most." He frowned. "Your kind hates us, Simeon. Hates us with such passion sometimes I shudder to think about it. Occupying your lands would only intensify that hate." He shrugged. "Besides, everything we've learned from the times when we've abused our own kind leads us to believe the only real solution is for you to free yourselves. We can help you along in a limited way. But you've got to find your own future."

I looked up at the ceiling. "Why didn't Sammy ever leave the Zone?" I asked after a time, though I already suspected the answer. "Or Mrs. Rudder either? After my parents died, I mean, and their plans went to shit?"

"Several reasons," the man explained, after a moment's thought. "One was guilt. Sammy in particular shouldn't have stayed Inside so long or so continually. He took insane risks and eventually ruined his health." The man sighed. "No one else could've done it, Simeon. Not another man who ever lived." Then he turned to face me again. "Mostly, he did it for you. He was your only stable parent."

I gulped, and my eyes began to burn. Deep inside I'd known the answer for many years. But now, for the first time, I'd heard it spoken aloud.

"There's a cynical way to look at it too. We desperately need someone like you, on more levels than you probably appreciate. You proved your kind is as intelligent and as educable as we norms, given decent support. But, far more than that, you're also a sort of bridge. A fur who understands how we norms look at the world, while at the same time being immersed in and a respected part of your own culture." He folded his arms. "God knows you've had it hard. A dozen Railroaders a year have come to me, begging to have you pulled out of the miserable, filthy jungle you were raised in, often in the name of simple humanity. And perhaps we should've done exactly that. But we had to think of all the other furs, too. The ones for whom you're the best hope, in the long term, we've ever had."

I closed my eyes. "You used me. Sammy used me, too."

"To a degree," the norm agreed. "And maybe to our shame. But..." I felt his bulk leaning over me, and when I re-opened my eyes his features were hard and cold. "My brother Sammy loves you like a son, Simeon. He lived without complaint in the jungle with you for year after endless year, when he could just as easily have climbed right back into the ivory tower and resumed his place at the top of his field. Or, more likely, been elected to an important office. He lived his entire life in such a way as to give you the best possible understanding of what makes the Zone tick and provide the most stable home he could manage, doing whatever he had to do to survive in the meantime. I don't know of anyone else in the world who could've kept himself alive so long under such conditions."

Brother? I thought to myself. Sammy was this man's brother? Sure enough, now that I'd been told I could see a definite resemblance. "You're my uncle?"

"Half-uncle, "he corrected me. "Sammy and I share the same mother." Then he smiled and extended his hand. "I'm pleased to finally meet you, Simeon. In way I already feel as if I've known you for years from reading your papers and such.

"My name is Ralph Emory, and I'm in charge of the Underground Railroad project."

# Chapter Thirty-Two

I had more family all of a sudden than I'd ever dreamed. Though it didn't take the 'bots long to fix me up, while I was still in bed a whole parade of visitors came by to see me. Most of them I didn't know. But Mrs. Rudder cried for almost an hour at my bedside, and once they let Fina in she wouldn't leave at all. The rest of the people were strangers, though they seemed to care about me a lot. They were important Railroaders who Ralph told me I didn't have to let in. But I did anyway, because I sort of suspected Sammy'd want it that way.

By the fourth day I was on my feet again and in some ways feeling better than I had before I was shot. That was when I got to go see first Shiv, who'd been medivacked right alongside me and was still in a coma, and then Sammy, who wasn't dead after all.

"What?" he roared when I sort of almost-cried and told him I'd thought he was gone. "You ungrateful little shit! Do you think I'm *that* easy to chill?" The 'bots were doing good work on him too. Though he was hooked up to a lot more hoses than I'd ever been, his color was better than in months and the film was gone from his eyes. We sat together for hours, sometimes talking about the Great Rumble and sometimes just sitting in silence, glad to be together. Finally, after one of the long silences, I asked him the question that'd been bugging me for so long. "Why?" I finally demanded.

"Why what?"

"Why'd you have me steal the autocannon? I mean... Look. I know now the Railroad's been propping you up for years. Helping you design gadgets, and shipping in parts through the tunnels and stuff like that."

He blushed. "I designed a lot of it myself." he protested. "And there also wasn't anyone to help me set it up. Or to teach *you* everything you know about making quality shit out of scrap parts, young man."

I smiled. "You're still the Wizard, at least in my book. But... Look. If you needed an autocannon, couldn't they have gotten you one? And what'd you need it *for*?"

Sammy's smile faded, and he eased his head back onto his pillow. "Well... I had you steal it for the same reasons I had you shoplift norm stores Outside and do other little jobs, Simeon."

"Which was?"

"In your culture, only criminals are respected. I wanted you to be a leader someday. The only way this could happen was for you to be a respected part of your culture. Besides, organizing a posse to commit crimes is fantastic leadership experience." He grinned like a little boy. " I can't imagine a better background for a politician, Inside or Outside. On the job training, sort of."

I snorted, and then my expression sobered again. "But *why*, Sammy? Why the cannon, when you had to know the shitstorm it'd unleash?"

Sammy's smile faded, and suddenly he looked old again. Then he turned towards the wall. "The shitstorm was coming anyway. There's been a fundamental power shift, one you still don't know about." He shook his head slightly. "Someone else was offering to sell Stone stenguns. We still don't know who, or what they were after."

My eyes narrowed. "Then why'd he want to keep me?"

"Because you're cheaper. And, as I'm sure you figured out, because eventually he could control you and thus his weapon supply." Sammy sighed. "Anyway, I designed the tank years back and kept it half-made just in case I needed it in a hurry."

I shook my head, still not understanding. "But..."

"That was for *you*," he explained, turning back to face me. "In case they took you hostage, which was looking more and more likely every day." He shook his head. "Son... I could always commit suicide if they took me. I've been wired up for it since before you were born. But to get you out of trouble, I needed mobile, heavy firepower. And I couldn't exactly wait until the last minute to come up with it, now could I?" He sighed. "But instead of them taking you, I got sick and became the weak link. Stone made his move on *me*." He shook his head again and grinned. "And you, you young idiot, came to the rescue, instead of the other way around."

He reached out to stroke my ears. He was still hugging me up close to his bed when Fina arrived. She'd been very quiet the past couple days. Even when I'd tried to initiate conversations, she'd not said much. Overwhelmed by her new surroundings, I supposed.

She smiled politely at Sammy, and then looked at me. "Simeon, Mr. Emory would like to see you in the conference room, if you feel up to it. Mrs. Rudder is with him. And so are a bunch of other norms." She looked a little scared. "They're all wearing suits, too."

I smiled back, and then wrapped my good arm around her. I'd been doing that a lot of late; it felt natural after we'd been through so much together. I looked down at Sammy. "Do you know anything about this?"

"Maybe, and maybe not. To be perfectly honest with you, they're not telling me much anymore. That's to avoid putting too much stress on my heart before it heals." He snorted. "As if they knew what *real* stress is!"

I smiled back. Stress did indeed have an entirely different meaning in the Zone. Then I squeezed Fina again. "All right, then. Let's go see what they want."

## Chapter Thirty-Three

Everyone stood as Fina and I entered the conference room, which I took to be a good sign. Sure enough, the only people I knew were Mrs. Rudder—who was standing proud and dressed more expensively than I'd ever seen before—and Mr. Emory, who was stationed at the head of the table. "Welcome, both of you." he declared as we came in. "Please be seated. Care for anything to drink?"

Everything seemed friendly enough, though Fina gripped my hand so tightly it hurt. She didn't understand the norm world nearly as well as I did, I suddenly realized. Despite her close association with Mrs. Rudder, she hadn't grown up with her the way I had with Sammy. Nor had she been required to read norm magazines and news-pages. In other words, she hadn't benefited from any of the thousand ways I'd absorbed norm culture with my breakfast greens. As a result, my girlfriend was nearly as terrified as she'd been while riding in the tank. It was this way with all furs, I now understood. And this was why I was a bridge. Part of the hatred was rooted in fear, which in turn was at least partly the result of extreme ignorance. That, at least, I'd overcome by virtue of my upbringing. So I squeezed Fina's hand as hard as she was squeezing mine, and smiled at her as reassuringly as I knew how. That seemed to help, at least a little. But still...

Two of the people in the conference room weren't wearing suits. They were wearing police uniforms, and didn't look at all happy. I glared at them icily, smiled Shiv's best smile, and then looked away.

"All right, then," Mr. Emory began, scowling. I wasn't sure if he'd noticed the little interplay or not. "Simeon and Fina, we have some serious issues to deal with here. Some of which can't be put off much longer." He looked expectantly at Mrs. Rudder.

"Simeon, dear," she began. "You've been through an awful lot. But Ralph's right. We don't have much time," She scowled. "A day or so at most. If things go a certain way, that is."

I nodded, but said nothing.

"First of all..." Ralph began, leafing through some papers, "we have some legal issues to deal with." He scowled, and then turned towards the police officers. "Are you *certain* that the charges can't be dropped? This is after all quite a remarkable case."

"Absolutely not!" the policewoman declared. Her uniform carried more gold braid than the other officer's. "The city prosecutor laughed at me when I relayed your suggestion. It's more than my career is worth to come back without Bolivar in custody." She glared at me.

"Hmm..." Ralph murmured, leafing through his papers again. Finally he pulled out a document decorated by dozens of colorful seals and ribbons. "How about you bring a copy of this back to her instead?" He passed it over, and the cop-lady's eyes about bugged out of her head. "The Railroad is nothing if not well connected."

"B-b-but," she sputtered. "H-H-He hasn't even been tried yet!"

"I know," Ralph agreed. "Customarily, pardons aren't issued until *after* a conviction. But..." He smiled. "What the heck? He's still a juvenile, legally speaking. Under these extraordinary circumstances, an exception can surely be made."

"He's a god-damned—" she began, and then bit the words off. "You haven't heard the last of this!"

"Nor have either you or for that matter Judge Matthews," Emory assured the officers as they leapt to their feet and stomped towards the door. "Tell me. Do you live in a house you can't possibly afford on your salary? Just like the Judge does?"

"Fuck you!" was her only reply, unless one counted the slamming door.

"And now," Emory continued, unperturbed, "we can get down to the *real* business of this meeting." He looked at me. "Simeon, as your teacher told you, we have some urgent decisions to make. There isn't much time."

"Why the hurry?" I demanded, Sammy'd always taught me never to rush an important decision without good reason.

"Because the longer we keep you two and Shiv out of the Zone, the harder it's going to be to come up with a convincing way to slip you back in." Suddenly, he looked old.

"You don't have to go," a younger woman declared. She'd come to visit me earlier, and had even brought flowers. I didn't remember her name. All I knew was that she was some muckety-muck in the Railroad. "There are dozens, more likely hundreds, of universities that would love to have you as a student, Simeon. They'd offer you room, board... A stipend, even." She smiled at Fina. "And eventually you as well."

Suddenly, my hand felt like it was caught in a vise.

"If you want to go to college, Simeon," Ralph agreed, meeting the young woman's eyes, "you're completely free to. You don't ever have to go back into the Zone except of your own free will."

"But...?"

"But," Ralph agreed, smiling at my gentle gibe just as Sammy would've. "There are other possibilities."

"If you go back," Mrs. Rudder explained, "you'll pretty much take Sammy's place in the greater scheme of things. Except that instead of just trying to walk the tightrope and play for time, like he did while you were growing up, we want you to take over."

"Clean up the Zone," Ralph agreed, "For the good of everyone, from within."

"The only way it *can* be done," Mrs. Rudder agreed.

"I...But..."

"You'd have plenty of support," Sammy's half-brother continued. "A whole team to help keep the gadgets going and stuff. We can sneak them in and out though the tunnels. You'd be surprised how much they can do to help out without ever leaving the privacy of your shop."

"You'd have funding, too," another man I didn't know added. "Damn near unlimited funding, in real-world terms." He leaned back in his chair, crossed his arms and shook his head. "The simple truth is, Simeon, we don't have anything else nearly so promising going for us. I thought Dr. Kiel was a lunatic, for trying to raise you in there. And perhaps even a child abuser as well. Now, I begin to understand his vision."

"You'll make a good salary," Mrs. Rudder promised. "And we'll give you a panic button. So you can be evacuated on short notice if things go badly."

I looked around the room. "You mean, you want me to... Take over the Zone and *fix* it?"

The young woman leaned forward. "You don't have to, Simeon. Some of us think it's a *terrible* idea." She leaned back and crossed her legs.

"Others of us," Mrs. Rudder declared, looking me directly in the eye, "think you're a lot of furs' best hope."

I looked up at the ceiling. "Forgive me," I said. "But let me put this plainly, in terms I'm comfortable with. This has got to be the most fucked-up load of shit I've ever heard in my life." I shook my head. "Have you got any *idea* what you're asking for?"

The young woman smiled, but said nothing.

"First," I continued, "no one's ever gonna trust me again. Not since I've been with you norms for almost a week now."

"How about if you were to escape from prison and sneak back in?" Ralph more suggested than asked. "That could be arranged easily enough. We could spread supportive rumors in promising places. Maybe you even, ah... *chilled* a couple guards on the way out?"

"...and then, there's the whole rumble-thing," I continued, ignoring Mr. Emory. "I still don't know who won. If it was the Avengers, I'd be dead before I took two steps."

"The Avengers lost," Mrs. Rudder answered calmly. "They're all gone. Or almost all of them are gone, at least. The Skulls are hunting down the survivors as we speak. Though not very effectively. There's an internal power-struggle going on, so the efforts are poorly coordinated."

"That's 'cause Shiv's here, on ice," I replied. "He was all set up to become The Man, and everyone knew it."

"He can come off of the ice," Ralph observed. "Any time we like. He can escape with you, even."

I rolled my eyes. "Like, he's gonna trust me, after this all this shit's gone down? You people really *don't* understand us furs, do you?"

"Maybe not," Mrs. Rudder replied. "Though I'm reasonably certain an answer to that little difficulty can be worked out, as well." She smiled.

"And then there's the ignorance, and the filth, and hatred..." I continued. "The stick, too. Most of all, the stick! Ain't no one gonna clean up jackety-shit, so long as there's stick on the street and furs in need."

Ralph sighed. "You're right there, Simeon. Absolutely, dead-on correct. But we're working on that, too."

Without my consciously willing it, my ears perked up. "Really?"
Emory smiled a wolf's smile. "Really."

"What would you say," Mrs. Rudder asked, "if a new kind of stick was for sale? One people could buy for almost nothing?"

"One that cured the need and didn't have side effects," Ralph continued. "But didn't make you high, either?"

I looked away. "People wouldn't buy it. They want the buzz!"

"Your friend Wiener would," a new voice interrupted. It was Fina, of all people.

"How on earth..." I objected. "I mean... You don't even know Wiener."

"Sure I do! He's my cousin. The one who told me the best way for me to get to know you was by helping out at the school." She smiled. "He looks up to you like... Well, I don't know what. A god, maybe. And he's scared, Simeon. Really deep-down scared. He knows what the stuff's doing to him."

"It's not ready yet," Mrs. Rudder explained. "We're at least a couple years away. Maybe even longer if the trials go badly. So it's not a sure thing."

"The pharmacists say the problem is devilishly complex," one of the suited men added. "We can't promise."

"But we can try," Mr. Emory said. "And hope."

"And pray." Mrs. Rudder smiled. "Plus be ready to distribute, if and when."

I pressed my lips together and though about all the evil shit I'd ever seen that was ultimately traceable to stick and the stick trade. Then I thought of Romeo, Peckerhead, and poor little Weiner, hanging around outside the chinkshop, in need and not able to do a damn thing about it.

Did Weiner really admire me that much, I wondered? Damn! And he didn't have all that much time left...

"So," I said finally. "How exactly can you make Shiv trust me? This I'm dying to hear...."

# Chapter Thirty-Four

*Two Months Later*

"...all the way down Chestnut," Growly was explaining, gesturing with a bejewelled hand. We were sitting at what'd become my usual table at The Warrens. "Business is almost as good as before. And profits are actually better, since that bastard Stonecold isn't taking a cut anymore."

I nodded and smiled as Shiv, taking his cue, did the same. You had to look close or else it didn't show. But as I nodded just the tiniest trace of tension erased itself from the big lion's features. He hadn't had anything to do with the hit on Sammy, he'd reassured me over and over again, once the dust was all settled. He'd been forced to cooperate with Stone and the Avengers, compelled totally against his will. His sob story was so convincing I might even have believed him, if it hadn't been for the Outside gun-supply thing. The rumored new source of guns that'd precipitated the Great Rumble, that was. I couldn't be certain. But Growly was already smuggling heaven-only-knew how much stick into the Zone. It made sense he'd be the one best-positioned and with the right contacts to bring in guns as well. As near as I could recall, Growl hadn't looked to me like he'd been under all that much duress at the time. But facts were facts and business was business. The sad truth was that my fellow furs would blow the roof off of the Zone in less than a week without Growly's illegal pharmaceuticals. The resulting eruption would make the Uprising look like a tea party. So for the time being I needed him and his filthy product as much as he needed Shiv's soldiers. Shiv, in turn, needed my stenguns. Eventually, with luck I'd be able to ease Growly out of the business by offering a much less destructive substitute, just as I was already slowing weapon deliveries to the Skulls. But it'd take time. Rome wasn't built in a day, and the Zone wasn't gonna get unfucked overnight, either. In the meantime my hands were as filthy as everyone else's, just as Sammy's had been before me. There simply wasn't any other way.

Shiv was another story altogether. He loved being The Man of the Skulls, even while wearing the invisible leash and collar the Underground Railroad people had padlocked onto him. A little magic box had been installed in his chest while he was unconscious, or so he'd been informed. Personally, I wasn't sure if it was all bullshit or not. While the Railroad was willing to push the limits ethics-wise, I didn't know if their balls were actually that brassy. Anyway, the truth was almost irrelevant because betting the box didn't exist was all downside for Shiv. He'd been told he could be effortlessly located and his ticket cancelled anywhere on the planet. If I caught a noodge or a stray slug or if any sort of evil accident were to befall me, he'd outlive me by minutes at most. Not that I figured he'd ever put it to the test. Sometimes a near-death experience genuinely changes a man, and I believed this to be the case with Shiv. Not being stupid, he understood the *real* reason he was getting less than a quarter of his old stengun allotment wasn't because I was really that crappy of a machine operator. He knew times were a-changin' and that he'd be a lot better off on the winning side of the program.

Shiv sank a lot of personal time and effort into helping Mrs. Rudder find a new location for her school, a much-larger one that was clean and well lit and, if harder to defend, under a lot less threat these days. He was also borrowing books, my ex-teacher had informed me with glee - the same high-quality literary shit he'd so loved back when he'd been my only rival as a Zone scholar. The Skullfuckers weren't going to go legit overnight; only a fool could believe that. But in a few months or years could they perhaps come far enough to serve as a sort of temporary police-force to maintain order during free elections? Just maybe, I reckoned. If we cleaned up the drug-money first, which was being worked on elsewhere and by greater minds. Until then all I could do was prepare the ground and hope.

And dance, of course. I could do that too, and pretty much anytime I wanted to nowadays. The band was just finishing its warmup when Growly rose to take his leave. Then Shiv grinned, and I nodded out towards the dance floor. "Shall we, Jeffrey?" I asked.

"Let's hit it, Simeon!" he agreed, smiling. His smile looked a lot better these days. The filed-off parts of his incisors hadn't quite grown all of the way out yet and wouldn't for some time. But there'd been real progress. "Look!" he declared, pointing towards the entrance where a whole gaggle of rabbits were arriving together. "Here comes Fina, out of school early." He waved. "Hello!"

"Hi, Jeffrey!" she replied as she came bouncing up. Then it was my turn. I got a hug and kiss instead of just a hello. I smiled and squeezed my best girl back. At the hospital, the night after the big meeting, we'd talked long and hard about many things, reaching not just one decision regarding our futures but many. One of them had been to try, at least for a little while, spending said futures together. So far it was working out very well indeed for both of us. Down in my workbench drawer was a pair of plain golden rings. I'd made them myself, from scraps Sammy'd saved and cherished over the years. It wasn't quite time yet. But soon, very soon...

And then the band was playing, the dancers were lining up, and The Warrens was hopping on yet another Saturday night, just one of an endless series of Saturday night dances that stretched as far back as anyone could remember and would continue on as far into the future as anyone could imagine. But this was *our* Saturday, *our* moment, *our* place in the great ebb and flow of history. And we were living our lives as we chose to live them.

For the first time ever, as we leapt and spun together, I began to know what it truly meant to be free.

www.ingramcontent.com/pod-product-compliance
Lightning Source LLC
Chambersburg PA
CBHW050801250626
47155CB00005B/2168